EXILES ON ASPERUS

John Wyndham was born in 1903. Until 1911
he lived in Edgbaston, Birmingham, and
then in many parts of England. After a wide
experience of the English preparatory
school he was at Bedales from 1918 to 1921.
Careers he tried included farming, law,
commercial art, and advertising, and he first
started writing short stories, intended for
sale, in 1925. From 1930 to 1939 he wrote
stories of various kinds under different
names almost exclusively for American
science fiction publications. He also wrote
detective novels. During the War he was
in the Civil Service and afterwards in the
Army. In 1946 he went back to writing.
His most famous novels are THE DAY OF
THE TRIFFIDS, THE KRAKEN WAKES
(both of which have been translated into
several languages), THE MIDWICH
CUCKOOS, (filmed as THE VILLAGE
OF THE DAMNED), and TROUBLE WITH
LICHEN. John Wyndham died in March 1969.

D1319761

**Also by the same author,
and available in Coronet Books:**

The Secret People
Stowaway to Mars
Wanderers of Time
Sleepers of Mars

Exiles
On Asperus

John Wyndham
Writing as
John Beynon

CORONET BOOKS
Hodder and Stoughton

Coronet edition 1979
Second impression 1980

Printed and bound in Great Britain for
Hodder and Stoughton Paperbacks, a
division of Hodder and Stoughton Ltd.,
Mill Road, Dunton Green, Sevenoaks,
Kent (Editorial Office: 47 Bedford
Square, London, WC1 3DP) by
Hunt Barnard Printing Ltd.,
Aylesbury, Bucks.

ISBN 0 340 24046 6

CONTENTS

Exiles on Asperus

FOREWORD

Whatever our private opinions – and they may differ a great deal – of the administration of Earth's colonies in the Solar System, we are, nevertheless, proud of their existence. Not only do we admire the men who founded them, but we are even prouder of the endurance of danger, hardship and discomfort by those who developed them. Few of us would care to spend even a week at a trading station upon Venus, yet many a man has worked for years in that eternal blanket of steamy mist, helping to increase Earth's comfort and wealth.

Not many of us would endure without protest a term of scorching by day and freezing by night upon the desert plains of Mars – that greatest of our colonies, so woefully mismanaged until the revolt of 2077, as to be like a stinging slap in the face of Justice. And still greater would be our trials if we should be forced to fight against the gravitation of the major planets.

Earth has cause, indeed, to be proud of all her colonies – all, that is, save one. The name of this one colony will be found in no directory; it is officially unrecognised. It is severed and will remain severed, probably forever, from its parent world. Its men hold no communication with us, and it is long since we have heard how they fared. A conspiracy of silence has closed down on its unfortunate existence, and one of our earliest – though involuntary – settlements is unknown to most Earthmen even by name. Its story is unique.

I

MISADVENTURE

A violent shock threw the navigator of the *Argenta* forward in his chair so that he sprawled across his control desk. His two companions in the navigating dome staggered and slid across the deck plates. The clangour of a dozen or more alarm bells jangled throughout the ship. Angus McDowell, the chief engineer, made his way back to the desk, ruefully rubbing that part of his head which had met the wall.

'What the hell – ?' he began in a mildly surprised tone. The third man, Joe Seely, scrambling from the floor, cut him short.

'Holed, sure as we're living,' he exclaimed. 'These ruddy asteroids! – where's the damage, David?'

The navigator turned to look up at the rows of indicators mounted to the left of his desk. In the middle of the top row a red light was winking briskly.

'Guard room,' he reported.

'Hell!' Joe, who was officer of the watch, tore out of the navigating dome and they could hear his voice bellowing orders down the corridor as he ran. Angus strolled closer to the desk. His was a lanky, angular figure possessed of long arms and big joints. He showed no smoothly rounded muscular development, but those who had once tried conclusions with his tough, sinewy frame seldom wished for more. A long faced Scotsman, this, who had never known Scotland. The product of ancestors bred in the shipyards of the Clyde; inheriting their engineering tradition with their blood. His manner towards the navigator was slightly paternal.

'Serious, Sonny?' he asked.

David shrugged his shoulders. A few years in the service had already given him a degree of that fatalism characteristic of so many space sailors.

'Final for those who happened to be in the guard room. That indicator means that they hadn't a chance to plug the leak. All their air was gone in two seconds. For the ship as a whole, not very serious.'

Angus nodded relievedly. 'Surprising it wasn't my engines. We do have a bit of luck – sometimes.' He paused before he added: 'Think I'll cut along and have a look at the mess.'

Angus clattered across the room, bending his head as he passed through the low exit. David returned to his calculations and corrections. No one was to blame for the accident. Approaching the asteroid belt, above the plane of the ecliptic, one could do no more than plot a course avoiding the larger, known fragments of rock, and trust to luck for the rest. Luck, on this occasion, had been less unkind than she frequently was.

Angus, making his way forward, towards the guard room, found a knot of men crowded around the entrance. Above the door, now automatically sealed by air pressure, a red danger light glowed steadily. Joe Seely was, with some difficulty, climbing into a space-suit and attempting to bawl his orders above the continued clamour of the alarms. As the bells abruptly ceased Angus heard him say:

'Six men to bring the portable airlock. Snap to it.'

The six raced off down the passageway while he still struggled with the intractable garment. When, at last, the stiff folds had been tugged up and the fasteners securely fixed, he picked up the air tanks and examined the dials. He dropped them disgustedly.

'Half pressure – criminal carelessness. Somebody's in for it over this. You!' he roared, startling a near member of the crew, 'new oxygen pack. Jump to it!'

He lifted the space helmet and, turning it over between his hands, examined it with caution.

'Hm. Appears to be satisfactory,' he admitted grudgingly.

Angus with a grin placed his big hand on the other's shoulder.

'Now, don't you get rattled, laddie,' he advised. 'Gettin' rattled never did a man any good. He forgets details if he gets all het up – and you only forget details once when you're in space.'

For a moment Joe seemed inclined to resent the warning. Then he smiled back and nodded. Angus was an oldtimer and privileged. Besides, he had spoken the truth: Joe had been getting windy.

The party returned bearing the portable airlock. It was in

the form of a hollow box built of steelium sheets, but it lacked one of the longer sides. Around the six feet by four of this missing part, it was heavily faced with rubber. In the side opposite the space was set a door. The men fitted the contrivance over the guard room door so that side flanges slid over bolts provided for the purpose. While they worked hard with spanners to secure it, another of the crew attached the pipe which would later exhaust the air. Joe watched fidgeting impatiently until the spanners were laid aside.

'Finished?'

'All correct, sir,' the leader assured him.

'Good. Give me a hand with this helmet.'

Half a minute later he was inside the lock. He made sure that all was in order and the door safely bolted behind him and gave the starting signal of three taps on the metal wall. The pointer before him began to back swiftly as the pump did its work. In a short time the pressure became low enough for him to open the guard room door and, with a rush, the remaining air dissipated into the vacuum.

Joe moved clumsily over the threshold and surveyed the room. It was not a pleasant sight. It was, in fact, far worse than he had expected. For one thing there had evidently been far more men in the room than was usual at any one time. Their lifeless bodies seemed everywhere. Sagging in their chairs, fallen forward across the tables or sprawled on the floor wherever the sudden going of the air had left them. Their faces were grey-blue and their mouths lolled open to show grey tongues.

Their fingers were tight clenched as though in a last, despairing clutch at receding life, and their eyes, fantastically protruding, seemed still to stare at death. The eyes of some had left their sockets. From the noses and ears of many, little streams of blood had spurted to be frozen by the cold of space. Joe felt sick. It was not the first time he had seen men dead from exposure to the vacuum, but it was the first time he had seen them in such numbers.

He counted more than thirty – almost the entire corps of guards snuffed out in a single moment. For what purpose they had all been assembled at once, he could not guess. He pulled himself together and brought his mind back to the practical aspect of the situation.

10

'It'll be tough work looking after the prisoners now,' he muttered.

He looked along the room and saw on the port side the three-foot hole which had caused the tragedy. Beyond, he could look out into space – a velvet blackness, pricked by distant stars. He turned to starboard in search of the corresponding hole and saw with a shock that there was none. He had never heard of a meteorite failing to pass clean through any ship it had struck. It became plain that here was a chance in several million. The object must have been moving at a speed but little different from their own. Its force at the angle of impact had only, therefore, been sufficient to carry it through one side of the *Argenta*. A short search for the cause of the mischief revealed it lying beside one of the corpses at the foot of a stanchion. The stanchion, massive member though it was, had been badly bent by the encounter. Joe whistled softly in surprise as he looked down. Instead of the irregular lump of cosmic rubbish he expected, he found himself gazing at a dented, steelium cylinder.

'A message rocket,' he muttered. 'Now what the – ?'

Bending down, he rolled it over and felt for the catch which would slide the message compartment cover aside. He found it and gave the necessary combined pressure and twist. The lid snapped back to reveal only a single sheet of paper which he snatched up hurriedly and stuffed into a pocket of his space-suit.

After a few more minutes of cursory examination of the room, he crossed to the wall and lifted down one of the emergency plates which must be carried in all rooms and cabins. Leaving this handy, he returned to the doorway and gave the signal taps for the admission of air. Then he hurried back to the plate and held it over the hole waiting for the air pressure to lock it into position with a weight of fifteen pounds to the square inch. It could not keep out the cold of space for the vacuum in that section of the double hull had been destroyed, but it would keep in the air and artificial warmth could be supplied for the time taken in repairs.

Some little time passed without result. Evidently there had been a hitch somewhere and again Joe began to grumble over the inefficiency of the *Argenta*'s crew as he waited for the valve to open. At last, however, the needle of the wall dial flickered and began slowly to turn. Soon it became unnecessary for him to hold the emergency plate. He turned off his air supply and removed his helmet as the pointer neared the fifteen mark. Then he strode over to the door of the lock. He began to speak angrily as he opened it, but the words died as he stared at a pistol ominously facing him.

'Both hands up, please,' said a voice quietly.

His helmet fell with a crash as his hands rose.

II

REVOLT

Joe emerged from the lock and looked wonderingly around the semi-circle of facing men. They were short, large-chested men with brown faces and hands. The meaning of the situation struck him with an unpleasant jolt.

'The Martians – the prisoners,' he exclaimed.

Thus did the widespread Martian revolt of 2077 affect even the *Argenta*, far out in space.

The man who held the pistol answered Joe.

'The Martians, yes, but it is you Earthmen who are the prisoners now.' His speech was both good and fluent though, like that of most of his race, he retained the characteristic lilt.

Joe could see Angus at the rear of the group, towering over his lessor captors. The Scotsman was manifesting no little irritation:

' – lot of lousy sons of misbegotten desert rats. You'll see what you'll get for this, you – ugh.' The speech ended in a grunt as a pistol jabbed uncomfortably in his ribs. Joe turned back to his captor.

'This is piracy. You know the penalty?'

The Martian smiled. 'This is more than mere piracy – it is revolution. Everywhere the Martians are turning upon their oppressors. You thought that we were crushed. You thought that you had stamped out the last spark of our spirit when at length you caught Sen-Su and condemned him and us to exile. That was a foolish thing to do. Our plans were already made. By the arrest of Sen-Su you gained us more support and lit

12

the fuse of the revolution. Every loyal Martian knew the date and the time.'

As he finished, another group approached down the corridor. Joe could see that it comprised most of the ship's officers including David Robbins, the navigator. One, however, he missed.

'Where is Captain Briscoe?'

'Unfortunately, he is dead,' admitted the Martian.

'If you killed him, you swine – ' began Angus.

The other shook his head.

'We did not. He succeeded in killing two of us, but when he saw that we had really got the situation in hand, he shot himself. It was a great pity. There would have been no dishonour for him to surrender.'

Joe believed him. He knew the old captain for a man of dogged pride; incapable of surrender while the means of death remained.

'And what's to be done with us?' he asked, hoping his uneasiness was not audible in his voice.

'For the present you will be confined in the officer's mess. Your crew is now occupying our cells.'

By this time the two groups had joined and were moving on together. At the door of the mess room they halted. Each of the seven officers was first searched for concealed weapons and then passed in. Finally the door was closed and bolted upon a very dejected group of men. Only Angus retained the spirit to express his opinion of the situation: it appeared to amount to a withering blast of non-repetitive profanity.

'All right, all right,' counselled Joe after a while. At another time he might have admired Angus's linguistic attainments, but at present they seemed unhelpful. 'Just forget the Martians' ancestors for a bit – they're dead, anyway. The trouble is, what're we going to do? We can't sit down under this.'

'Do? What the hell can we do? I don't mind telling you it's the last time I ship on a ruddy convict carrier. What sort of filthy mess are they making of my engines, I wonder? A lot of stinking, bladder-chested – '

'Oh, cut it out. Have we got any weapons?'

David jerked open a drawer which he remembered to have contained a pair of pistols. It was empty. A search of the room soon revealed that the Martians had been over it in anticipation of their hopes.

13

'Hm, they're no fools.' Joe noticed the door at the other end of the room. 'Try that door, David.'

David walked across and rattled the handle vainly. He shook his head.

'They seem to have caught us properly,' he admitted. 'What puzzles me is how they worked it. They can't have known that we were going to be holed.'

'No. That must have been just luck,' Joe agreed. 'Judging from what the man with the gun said, it was all pre-arranged. The guards being wiped out meant that they caught us sitting instead of having to fight. But I'd like to know just how they got out.'

As he spoke, he had been unfastening the space-suit which still encumbered him. He struggled awkwardly out of it and threw it into a corner. Torrence, the first officer, had made no comment since the calamity. Now he began to speak. Since the death of the captain, he became senior officer and, therefore, in command; none of those present had seemed to appreciate this, and his tone showed his resentment. He was unfortunate in that a peremptory knocking at the door cut him short half-way through the first sentence. All the men turned surprisedly. This seemed an unusual courtesy to prisoners.

'Unbolt this door at once,' demanded a Martian voice while its owner rattled the handle.

David was about to call out that it was already unbolted, but, at a sign from Angus, he stopped. The Scotsman rose swiftly from his chair and lifted it above his head. He crossed the room and posted himself behind the door.

'It's not bolted,' he called.

He braced himself, ready to crash the chair upon the head of the first comer. The rest prepared to spring for the fallen man's weapon and charge the door.

Disconcertingly, a voice addressed them from behind.

'Ah,' it said, 'a little reception committee. I thought there might be, so I took the precaution of entering by the other door.'

They all whipped round to face a Martian who was accompanied by armed guards. Angus shamefacedly lowered his chair. The newcomer was short, even for his race, but his proportions were excellent, and in his carriage was a dignity utterly different from the frequent pomposity of small men. A

14

slight smile crossed his clean-cut face at the sight of their surprise.

'A little ruse of mine,' he explained.

'Who are you, and what do you want?' Torrence demanded curtly.

'My name, probably familiar to you, is Sen-Su. Till lately I was one of your prisoners.'

'The Martian nationalist?'

'Yes, and no doubt you have all heard many unpleasant things about me – probably are wondering what particular form of torment I have in store for you. They have made quite a bogy of me on Earth; I assure you they exaggerate. It has been a Governmental policy to malign me – Governments have to create thorough-going villains. In private life we should call them liars, but in public life they are propagandists.'

'Well?' Torrence attempted to make it clear from his tone that he was prepared to waste very little breath and time with a man of an inferior race.

'I have come primarily to express my regret at the death of Captain Briscoe. I assure you I regard it as a serious stain on an otherwise successful coup.'

There was no immediate reply from the Earthmen. They had not been taught to believe that Martians held to such a standard of behaviour. In fact, it was frequently stated that no Martian knew the meaning of the word 'honour'. David studied the little brown man and saw sincerity in his eyes. There was no mistaking the real thing. Moreover, many times in the past he had doubted that the Martians were such scum as Earth, in general, credited them with being. He looked around at his silent comrades and took it upon himself to reply.

'We thank you for that,' he said.

Angus, after a puzzled stare leaned over towards him.

'I believe you're right, Sonny,' he confided in a hoarse whisper. 'He means it.'

Torrence cut in with a sharp demand to know Sen-Su's intentions. The other raised his eyebrows at the tone, but his voice remained even as he answered:

'That is simple. Our parts are reversed. For you, the fate which was to be ours: for us, the occupations which were yours.'

'You intend to maroon us on the planetoid, Asperus?'

As Sen-Su nodded Torrence broke out wrathfully:

15

'You won't get away with that. All the ships in the Solar system will be at your heels. Far better surrender quietly now.'

Sen-Su smiled again, tolerantly.

'I see you do not yet understand. This is no isolated reversal for Earth. It is a fight for liberty. Everywhere, save on Earth itself, Martians have by this time risen in thousands, determined as only a persecuted people can be, to end Earth's oppression. You came to Mars and found an old race – old, before yours began. We were prepared to be friendly, but you let loose your adolescent cruelty upon us. You could not understand that a people may outgrow the futilities of war and strife. You called us decadent and weak.

'This impression, coloured with fictitious stories of our vices, was suggested again and again to all Earthmen, and, such is the immense power of suggestion scientifically sustained we became to your minds, monsters of depravity. The truth – that we were an old race, resting as a man rests when his work is done – was not allowed to percolate into your thoughts. You have disturbed our content; stirred us from our peace, and your oppression has meant our rejuvenation. Old Mars has had to arise in all her ancient might against alien barbarians.'

The first officer stepped forward with fists clenched.

'Barbarians? *You* call *us* barbarians?'

Pistols waved him back. Sen-Su shrugged his shoulders.

'If a demonstration of barbarity were needed, you have given it. You react like an animal.'

'But you cannot hope to subdue Earth and all her millions,' Joe objected. 'For one thing, there are not enough of you.'

'True. And that is not our intention. For one thing, it would be as barbarous as your treatment of us. We merely refuse to let ourselves and our planet be further exploited for one-sided gain. Now, I will leave you – I have important matters to attend to. I trust that I have made the situation clearer.'

The Martian party retired leaving an astounded group of prisoners behind them. The situation had indeed been made unpleasantly clear. Sen-Su's manner and restraint in itself had been a shock to men who had been taught to consider all Martians as mere semi-civilised degenerates who should be thankful to Earthmen for introducing the strong hand of control. His moderation was a contradiction of all their schooling. Torrence expressed his ill-controlled anger in threats. Angus, for once, was silent. He looked thoughtful.

'You know, Sonny,' he remarked after a while to David, 'I've got a feeling that there's a deal in what the man said.'

David nodded his agreement.

'I know. I've got that feeling, too. Of course, we always have been told what swine the Martians are, but how much of that is just politics? Has any of us here every really known the Martians?'

Torrence looked across and became conscious again of his position as first officer. His anger, moreover, had not abated.

'So that's the way of the wind? Not only is our ship seized by pirates and our captain killed, but we have traitors among our own officers.' His voice was truculent. 'Well, we know how to deal with traitors, don't we, boys?'

He looked around as he finished the question, but the response was curiously half-hearted. Most of the men turned their gaze aside rather than meet his. Angus stared at him with a pair of cold, hard eyes.

'You're a fool – but for that, I'd knock your rotten teeth and your insults down your throat together. I'm every bit as much against the Martians as you are, but that's no reason for fooling myself with a deck of lies.'

'You're calling me a liar?' Torrence rose.

'It seems to me we've all been hearing or telling lies about Mars, but that doesn't say I'm backing the Martians. If somebody in the Solar System has to get a bad deal, I'm still going to do my best to see it's not Earth.'

'You were talking sedition,' Torrence retorted doggedly. 'You and Robbins, there. As senior officer it is my duty – '

Angus had crossed and stood over the other, his long arms swinging ready.

'Your duty is what? You miserable little half-baked, wooden-headed – '

Joe Seely hurried to intervene. He swiftly retrieved the paper he had stowed in the space-suit pocket and waved it at the rest.

'Say, here's a bit of news for you,' he called loudly. 'That thing that broke into the guard room wasn't a meteorite – it was a message rocket.'

They all turned incredulously. Message rockets, as they all very well knew, had been banned by government decree for over twenty years.

'You mean to say the thing lodged aboard us?' David asked.

'I do, and here's the message.'

Joe unfolded the paper carefully and laid it on the mess table. The others, forgetful of the brewing fight, came clustering round him.

'The fellow who invented those things ought to have been sent off in one himself,' said Angus. 'It's a safe bet they've wrecked more ships than they've ever saved.' He leaned over Joe's shoulder and peered down at the sheet.

The date at the head was the fourteenth of August in the year A.D. 2052 – twenty-five years ago. For that quarter of a century the message rocket, having missed its objective, had been floating aimlessly in space, to end by causing the death of thirty and more good men. It was no wonder the devices had been banned. The message was brief, but plain:

'*Rocket ship*, RED GLORY (*C.O.* 1009), *passenger liner bound from Earth to the Moons of Jupiter. Disabled in the asteroid belt, and wrecked by forced landing upon planetoid believed to be Asperus. 300 survivors. Radio out of commission. Send help.*'

The signature at the foot read: '*James Stuart* (*Captain*)'.

Angus bent down to look more closely and assure himself that there was no mistake.

'Old Jamie, by the Lord. It's a small system. Does anyone remember a rescue from Asperus?'

No one did.

'Then it's odds on he's there still – if he's alive.'

'If they navigate properly, we should make Asperus in a couple of days,' remarked David. 'And, by the look of things at present, we'll have plenty of time to make a search.'

III

ON ASPERUS

The imprisoned officers crowded to the windows as the *Argenta* slowed for landing by circling about Asperus. The planetoid, although larger than Eros, had been discovered later, possibly because its orbit is almost circular while Eros, travelling his very oval path comes close to the Earth at times. Another difference between them is that Asperus is a spherical body while Eros, strangely enough, is not.

The name, 'Asperus', denotes, as it should, a world craggy and broken to the last degree of roughness, but it carries also a suggestion of barren severity which is entirely misplaced. On the contrary, vegetation is profuse.

As they watched the tumbled landscape far beneath, David gave such scraps of information as he could dig out of his memory. The diameter, he told them, was just under five hundred miles, though the density of the core was many times greater than that of Earth. The period of rotation was almost exactly twelve hours, and its year, 1,600 earth-days in length. Geographically he could tell only that it possessed two large seas, much broken with islands. But the men paid him little attention, they were far too interested in examining for themselves the world which must support them for an indefinite length of time.

Profuse is an inadequate word to describe the vegetation which clothes this pocket planet. They could see all the land wrapped in a green blanket from which, here and there, only the craggiest of spires pierced upwards in their rocky nakedness. Foliage sprang from every pocket of soil, bushes waved atop the most unlikely peaks and festoons of swaying creepers hung down from the ledges like green waterfalls pouring into the still denser growths below. Occasional gleams of water showed where steep-sided clefts had succeeded in trapping miniature lakes, and, infrequently, there occurred larger, shadowed valleys which could show level ground dotted with not inconsiderable trees. As the *Argenta* swept nearer still, a half-checked exclamation burst from Angus. He pressed closer to the window.

'What is it?' asked Joe, beside him.

But Angus made no reply. For the present he was keeping to himself the knowledge of a bright, metallic glint which had flashed from one valley. He marked the spot mentally by the queerly twisted crag which dominated it.

The ship, now travelling slowly, searched for a landing. A few moments later she was sinking gently to a green spread berth. Joe voiced the general sentiment as they touched.

'Well, we might be in a worse hole. There's certainly no desert here like there is on most of Eros. Even the mountains don't seem so high when you get the right proportions – nothing like Earth's mountains although they're so broken.'

Doctor Cleary, the medical officer, surveyed the scene less kindly. It would probably, he thought, mean a lot of work for him; this transferring of species to an alien world was not always the simple matter it appeared. But he made no comment; optimistic men are healthier than pessimists.

An audible bustling began to take place about the ship. There came a clang as the exit ramp was lowered. They watched the twenty-eight members of the crew march out under an escort of armed Martians, and turned sharply as the door of the mess room was flung open.

'This way!' ordered a sing-song voice.

They were conducted first to their cabins where it was permitted, under supervision, to collect such personal belongings as they might wish to take, and thence to the open. Sen-Su, personally supervising the expulsion, regarded them negligently as they passed him, but as they stepped off the ramp, he gazed more intently and a line appeared between his brows.

'Fu-Tan,' he called, 'how many officers are present?'

'Six, sir.'

'There should be seven.'

The man addressed as Fu-Tan looked puzzled for a moment, then:

'The tall man, the engineer, is missing,' he said.

'Find him at once.'

It was a mystery how Angus had managed to slip away. Neither the Martians nor his companions had noticed his going. Fu-Tan raised his lilting voice in orders. The business of unloading supplies for the exiles was suspended while all but a handful of guards joined in the hunt. It proved brief, for the *Argenta* was deficient in good hiding places. An approaching hubbub in the corridors soon suggested that the escaper had been caught, muffled broadsides of blistering blasphemy tended to confirm the suggestion. Angus, still muttering and cursing, appeared at the head of the ramp and was hustled down. Sen-Su smiled at his angry face.

'No stowaways on my ship,' he said.

Angus's reply was unprintable but had the other looked a little more closely he might have discerned an unaccountable gleam in the engineer's eyes.

The unloading of food and medical supplies was resumed.

Reports on Asperus stated that edible fruits grew abundantly so that the preserved food was more of a luxury than a necessity. When all the cases had been stacked, each man was given a broad-bladed, razor-edged knife some eighteen inches long.

The guards filed back into the ship. The ramp was withdrawn and its covering port made firm. A preliminary roar came from the rocket tubes. The *Argenta* lifted a trifle by the bows, then, with a blast of power, she was gone, climbing on a steep slant into the heavens. Gloomily the stranded Earthmen watched her shrink.

'Well, it can't be for long,' said David, at length. 'Once they find that Sen-Su's in circulation again, they'll realise what's happened and send for us.'

'And a pretty pack of fools we'll look,' returned Joe. 'The marooners marooned . . . What the devil's the matter with you?'

Angus, to whom the last part of the remark was addressed, was emitting a series of explosive grunts, suspiciously like laughter.

'Well, for a queer sense of humour, commend me to a Scot. What's so damned funny about this, I'd like to know?'

Angus got a hold on himself. 'Sen-Su thinks he's marooned us.'

'Not a bad think, either.'

'Yes, but he can't get away. I wasn't trying to stow away. I got along and opened the draining valves. He's not got enough fuel left to get clear. Our job was to dump him and his bunch, and we've done it in spite of them.'

'I'll be . . . So that was your little game. Angus, you're a genius.' Joe slapped him on the back.

The spirits of the whole company rose. Even though they had lost their ship and had been stranded, Angus had saved them from falling down on the main job. After a hurried discussion, it was decided to put some distance between themselves and the valley. When the Martians should notice their supply dials, it was considered likely that they would head back there, and no one was anxious to try conclusions with a shipload of angry Martians. The next question arose over the direction to be taken.

'I suppose one way's as good as another?' asked Joe.

'No,' Angus advised. 'Down to the south of this I saw something as we came over, and I'm willing to bet it was the wreck of the *Red Glory* or some other ship.'

'Taking a lot on yourselves, aren't you?' suggested Torrence. 'I'd just like to remind you again that I am in command here.' He looked round to see how this information was received. The men's expressions told him little. No one wished to mutiny, but if it came to a choice of leadership between a man promoted through influence, and one who had roughed the ether for many a year, they knew which to prefer. Joe Seely set himself to manage a tactful interposition with the result that the party moved to the south under the nominal leadership of the first officer, and the practical guidance of Angus.

Travel across Asperus was a curious sensation for Earth-bred men. Those with experience of planetary exploration managed to adapt themselves in short time to the low gravitation, but the novices continued to overshoot their aims again and again before they learned to gauge truly the amount of effort required. It was exasperating for these tyros to be carried sailing past their objectives by ill-judged bounds, but there was little danger of harm since descent seemed a matter of floating down rather than of falling. For half an hour Angus set a stiff pace, launching in a series of powerful leaps over such country as would have baffled all but the most skilful climbers had they had to contend with earthly gravitation. He noticed that the mountains were pitted with frequent caves, some obscured by screens of bushes and creepers, but others showing as stark, black holes in naked rock faces. The thought struck him that they might prove useful hiding places in case of pursuit. There was some grumbling from the rear about the unnecessary speed, but Angus knew what he was about. He was convinced that the *Argenta* would make for the valley where she had set them down, and his ears were wide open.

At the first mutter of distant rockets he gave the order to take cover and they crouched in the bushes, watching the ship as she swung like a silver shuttle above them. She sank slowly down behind crags they had already crossed. Angus gave the 'all-clear', and moved on in fantastic, flying leaps towards the south.

Night fell with surprising suddenness. Angus had hoped to reach the wreck while daylight lasted, but Asperus's swift revolution whisked the shrunken, distant sun out of sight while the rugged landmark was still several miles ahead. They were

22

left without light save for the sheen of accompanying asteroids and the glimmer of far-off constellations, almost unaltered. Travel over such country became well-nigh impossible.

Torrence suggested that the short night should be spent in one of the many caves, and Angus offered no objection. They had secured a good lead over the Martians and, even were their trail to be discovered, little or nothing could be done until dawn. One of the men reported a large cavern a few yards back. Torrence found it and led them into the gloom; his sword-like knife ready to his hand.

Angus struck a match, carefully shielding its rays from the entrance. By the flicker they could see a floor some twelve feet across and so dry as to be dusty, stretching back into the body of the mountain until it became lost in the blackness. The sides curved up into an arched roof five feet above their heads.

'Excellent!' pronounced Torrence briskly. 'It is dry, the entrance is not likely to be discovered and it is easily defensible.'

Angus started to speak and then restrained himself. The first officer was touchy and would certainly take any objection as a new attempt to belittle his dignity. Nevertheless, the engineer was uneasy though he would have been hard put to adduce any reason for his misgiving. Perhaps he had inherited a lingering fear of those hobgoblins and gnomes who had, according to legend, so sorely harassed his Celtic ancestors. Whatever the reason, it caused him to lie close to the entrance. Soon the sense of disquiet passed and he, like the rest, save for the sentry at the cave mouth, was asleep.

He awoke with a start. His hand already gripping the knife by his side. From somewhere came the whispering swish of a faint, ghostly movement. He looked towards the entrance and half started up. The sentry was no longer standing silhouetted on the ledge. A faint shuffling on the other side brought him round, trying vainly to pierce the wall of darkness. Stealthily he drew his feet up and settled the long knife more firmly in his hand. A scrape and the clatter of a loose stone jerked his head back to the entrance, and he drew a sudden breath. Black figures were stirring; indistinct outlines against the dark sky. Moving shadows: not the short Martians he had half expected, but grotesque, shrouded figures, six feet and more in height.

IV

A SUDDEN DISCOVERY

It was no time for inquiry; the vanished sentry told enough. Already a pair of the creatures were within the entrance. He could see them bending ominously above his sleeping friends. With whirling knife he leapt silently upon them. He felt the keen edge bite home and, simultaneously, there came a cry. A scream, but a scream no human throat could give; a mournful ululation with a harsh stridency which shredded the silence.

Confusion broke loose. The men sprang up, startled, yet bemused with sleep, and groping for their knives. The black prowlers retreated before Angus's circling blade, making headlong for the open. Twice more he felt the steel cleave deep before he gained the cave-mouth. The air sang in his ears with the shrill screams of alarmed and injured creatures.

He saw a half-dozen launch themselves into space as he came out upon the rocky ledge. Black forms which fell for a moment and then spread monstrous wings to check the fall. He watched them move in slow, powerful beats as the creatures rose and banked. Not for an instant did they check their desolate cries. Harshly the sound echoed in the shadow-hidden valley beneath and from further and yet further crags sprang answering cries like the wailing of funereal despair. A crescendo of screeching lament tortured the still night to pandemonium.

Mixed with the shrilling came the hoarser cries of striving men. Behind Angus a crowd of milling figures struggled and slashed in the dark, combating invisible opponents. With a stentorian command he dispersed the panic of their rough awakening and shook them into reality. They lowered their weapons and stood alert, breathing hard. From the dark, mysterious tunnel behind came the sounds of hurried feet mingled with those of occasional cries eerily echoing against the walls; sounds which grew fainter as their makers fled into the rocky heart of the mountain.

'What – what were they?' Torrence's dignity had fallen away and his voice was shaky.

Angus made no reply. Instead, he struck a light and counted the white, startled faces about him.

'Twenty-seven.'

Nobody commented, but a number of heads turned to let their owners gaze fearfully into the blackness whither two officers and six men had passed to an unknown fate.

'And Davie, and the rest are at the mercy of these blasted things – whatever they are,' growled Angus.

With the dawn they were able to examine the bodies of two of the assailants Angus had felled. They were bipeds, and that together with the disposition of organs common to most mammals, gave the impression that they were at least semi-human. Other characteristics did their best to counteract the impression. The creatures were a dull, metallic grey in colour, tall, thin and fragilely made. Attenuated arms, so long as to reach almost to the feet, were linked to the legs by enormous spans of membranous wings. Their only weapons appeared as cruelly curved claws at both the fore and hind tips of the wings. The size and shape of their half-human heads seemed to suggest an intelligence of some order. High enough, at least, to embarrass seriously a small party armed only with knives.

Nevertheless, Angus wished to lead a rescue party. He was dissuaded only with difficulty. The others managed, at last, to convince him that it would be more than foolhardy under the circumstances to attempt the exploration of the unlit caverns containing unknown numbers of the winged creatures. David Robbins, Doctor Cleary and the six men with them must be abandoned for the present, at least. When – and if – they should discover the *Red Glory*, they would have a stronghold, and – they hoped – weapons.

'The best thing we can do now,' said Joe, in conclusion, 'is to get right along, before those Martians get busy. They're sure to be on our tracks after that hullabaloo last night. We've got to settle with them before we can get a line on these flying screechers – the betting is that our men are safe for a while, if they're not dead already.'

For an hour Angus led on, leaping prodigiously, climbing and scrambling through valleys choked with foliage and up precipices whose faces were hidden behind thick tresses of creeper. If he had any doubt of the direction, any uncertainty, no suspicion of it was allowed to appear. They paused only once. Beside a stream in one of the lesser valleys, a man caught his foot in something which rattled drily. He jumped back with a cry which caused the rest to stop short.

'What is it?' Joe called.

'A skeleton, sir,' the man reported.

Joe came back. He saw at a glance that the bleached bones were human. Tangled among the ribs, he caught a glint of metal and drew out a slender chain on which swung an identity disc.

'Will Fording, Chicago, Radio Operator, *Red Glory* (C.O. 1009),' he read.

He picked up the rifle which lay beside the remains. It was utterly useless and caked in the rust of many years' accumulation.

'Poor devil – wonder what got him?' he murmured.

He dropped the gun and slipped the identity disc in his pocket. The party went on its way slightly chastened. So far they had encountered no sign of native animal life beyond the grey creatures and a few insects. The radio operator might have died of sickness or accident – it was impossible to guess with the little they knew of this queer planetoid.

An hour later, they breasted the final rocky ridge to gaze down on a sight which brought excited exclamations from them all. Close to the far side of a valley somewhat larger than any they had yet encountered lay a space ship of antiquated design. Her untarnishable plates still glittered in the sunlight, but half surrounding her were deep growths of a sturdiness which told that it was many years since she had sunk to this, her final, berth.

Angus's sharp eyes picked out the name *Red Glory* inscribed in faded letters upon her prow; beneath, half obscured by branches, he could make out a part of her Chicago registration number. But it was not the sight of the ship which had caused the party's surprise. They had expected no less. Their exclamations were due to the fact that the undergrowth before the entrance port had been cleared away. A broad path let from the ship to several acres of cultivated plots beside the stream which wandered down the centre of the valley.

Joe, for one, felt a rush of relief. Since the previous night's encounter he had been aware of growing doubts that any of the *Red Glory*'s complement could have survived.

'*Red Glory*, ahoy,' yelled Angus.

No voice replied though he fancied he saw a flicker of movement at one of the cabin windows. There was no wave of a welcoming arm such as he had expected. They hastened down the steep wall and across the valley floor. Midway up the cleared track to the open port, a voice called them to halt. Before and behind them figures oddly clad in rough materials stepped from the concealing bushes. All were men, and all held rifles trained upon them. A young man – Angus estimated his age at twenty-three or four – stepped forward and approached with wary suspicion.

'Who are you, and where do you come from?' he asked.

Torrence replied, and the young man watched him intently as he spoke. He seemed slightly at a loss. As he began to reply a figure made its appearance in the entrance of the *Red Glory*. An old man who stooped, and whose white hair hung down upon the shoulders of his coarse woven coat, but who still gazed with keen eyes from a weather beaten face.

'Jamie!' cried Angus. 'Jamie, don't you know me?'

The old man's face cracked into a smile.

'Aye, Angus, lad, it's you all right. Come along in and bring your friends with you.'

With one hand he waved away the riflemen who appeared bewildered, but retreated obediently.

'Well I'll be damned,' muttered Joe, 'does he think we've just dropped in to supper?'

Angus grinned.

'You could never surprise old Jamie – no one ever has.'

Accompanied by the riflemen who had not entirely lost their suspicion, the party filed aboard the ship.

They entered the main living-room to see a group of girls arranging baskets of strange Asperian fruits on the tables.

'Ye'll be wantin' some food, I doubt,' said Jamie. 'And ye can talk while ye eat. We heard your rockets yesterday,' he continued. 'The first rockets I've heard in twenty-five years – man, it was grand; like music.'

As the tale of the *Argenta* was told, more and more men and women and a number of children came crowding into the room. With some surprise Joe noticed the predominance of youth. There might have been perhaps thirty persons of middle age, and a few besides Jamie of advanced years, but the rest fell, almost without exception, below the twenty-four level. A number of them were introduced including the suspicious young man who had waylaid them. He, it transpired, was Andrew Stuart, son of old Jamie. Greta, one of the most attractive of the girls, was his wife.

Jamie heard their story through with little comment, but at the end he called Andrew to him and directed that a scouting party should be sent out. He looked a little worried as he turned back.

'We've got to keep these Martians away,' he said. 'Tis a pretty situation – they've got a good ship and no fuel, while we've got a useless ship, but there's plenty of fuel in her tanks yet.'

'Have you got rifles for us?' asked Angus.

'Aye, and pistols – more than we can use.'

Angus looked surprised, but a look in the old man's eye checked his question. He decided that Jamie had been doing a little gun-running as a sideline, and would not relish enquiries. Instead, he asked:

'What about your story? And what about these flying things? We're all sort of mazed.'

Jamie began his history from the disablement of the *Red Glory*. They had run into a meteor shower and had been lucky in not being carved to bits. Happily most of their score of leaks had been small, but the radio had been demolished and the relief operator who was in the room at the time, killed. One mixing chamber for gases had been wrecked, putting a number of tubes out of action.

They had set about limping for the nearest approaching body which they had believed to be Asperus. And, thanks to the low pull of the planetoid, managed a successful, if ungraceful landing. Thereafter a number of message rockets had been dispatched without result. The exact number of survivors, including passengers and crew, had been three hundred and seven.

In those first days Asperus had seemed a not unkindly place. It produced the necessities of life in abundance, and there was a feeling that fate might have been far more severe. Then, a week after the landing, fifty of their number, many of them women, disappeared. A search party was sent out and never seen again. Up to this time they had seen nothing of the grey, winged creatures which they later came to call by the name of 'Batrachs'. A second search party met a similar fate and still more of the survivors disappeared until, at last, Jamie had taken a firm stand.

Every sunset the door of the *Red Glory* was closed and locked and remained thus until dawn; nobody, under any circumstances, being permitted to go out by night. The numbers had now been reduced to sixty-five, omitting children. The Batrachs made bolder by their captures had besieged the ship for several nights, but, finding it impregnable, at last abandoned the practice. For several years now no member of the *Red Glory* colony had set eyes on a Batrach.

The creatures were strictly nocturnal in their surface operations, and the men became no less strictly diurnal. From that time the little colony had begun to prosper. Jamie from his position as captain had slid to the status of patriarchal ruler.

'But these Batrachs?' enquired Angus. 'You had guns to fight them with?'

'Yes, we had guns,' Jamie nodded, 'but so had the expeditions and they never came back. After all, laddie, a gun, even if it fires rocket shells, is at a disadvantage in the dark, and the Batrachs don't come in ones or twos, but in thousands. You were lucky last night; the only reason you are here now is that they didn't expect you. If they had been prepared – ' He spread expressive hands and shook his head.

V

TO THE RESCUE

Sometimes, Jamie admitted, he had thought of leading out yet another search party, but it was his duty to stay with his ship and protect the survivors to the best of his ability. There had been marriages. Jamie, as captain, had performed them, even his own. He had now become, he said proudly, not only the father of two boys and two girls, but a grandfather as well. The Batrachs, in his opinion were the only unhealthy things about Asperus; all the children of the colony had flourished

29

though he considered them slightly underdeveloped muscularly by reason of the lesser gravitation.

Angus, seeing that the story was tending to become a family history, pulled him back to the subject of Batrachs. Couldn't Jamie give more details about them? What did they do with their prisoners? What was their level of intelligence? Did they ever use weapons? He extracted little. Jamie considered them almost equal to men in intelligence – save that they never used weapons; of their treatment of prisoners he could say nothing, for no one had ever returned to tell. His tone showed plainly that he thought no one would, but Angus had different ideas on that subject.

Talk was cut short by the return of a scout who reported that the Martians were encamping in the next valley. Thoughts of rescue were temporarily put aside. Sen-Su and his little lot must be settled first.

First officer Torrence again emerged from that oblivion to which events seemed to condemn him. He proposed a sniping party. The suggestion met with a cold reception which genuinely astonished him. Angus was particularly incensed.

'This is not a murder gang. Our orders did not extend beyond marooning a bunch of political prisoners. They didn't ill treat us when we were at their mercy –'

'They're nothing more than a lot of damned pirates, and the penalty for piracy is death.'

Angus kept his temper with difficulty.

'That's as may be. If they had been real pirates, we'd now be so many corpses floating out there in space. I, for one, refuse to shoot them down in cold blood. They treated us well.'

'They murdered Captain Briscoe.'

'That's a lie!'

'This is mutiny.' Torrence's eyes were gleaming. He turned as though to appeal to old Jamie, but Angus cut him short.

'I don't care if it's sacrilege – I'm not going to do it. Get that?'

Joe joined Angus. He, too, preferred mutiny to murder. Torrence glared helplessly. The odds were against him and he was wise enough to know that the men would back Angus in any dispute. He could do no more than give in with bad grace. The party would stay in the *Red Glory* and let the enemy fire the first shot, if shots there must be.

'It's checkmate,' said Angus. 'Sen-Su will realise that mighty soon. Jamie tells me there are plenty of supplies aboard and they couldn't get us out for months. My only worry is that if they keep us cooped up here we shan't be able to find out what's happened to Davie and the others.'

All the men of the colony were called in for safety's sake. There was little over an hour of the short Asperian day remaining, and there was the risk of their being cut off by a party of Martians. Once or twice glimpses were caught of the little brown men on the escarpment of the farther side, apparently bent on reconnaissance.

'Cooping up' seemed to be the programme, for when Torrence went to the entrance port with a rifle in his hands, the warning smack of a bullet on the steel side above him caused his hasty retreat. Angus grinned when he heard of it.

'Teaching the sniper a few tricks, are they?' he said.

Night closed in without any further signs of activity. The port of the *Red Glory* was swung to and locked by old Jamie in the manner of one performing a ceremony. All sound of the outer world was shut away. The Martians could do what they liked: no portable weapon would be capable of making so much as a dent in the space ship's armour.

Angus awoke with a hand shaking his shoulder. He looked up to find Joe bending over him.

'Blast you, what's the matter?' he mumbled sleepily.

'Looks like a deputation. Get your clothes on and come along.'

Dawn had just broken and from the windows of the living-room they could observe three Martians who stood looking towards the ship. They had reached the beginning of the cleared pathway and were plainly ill at ease. The central figure upheld a stick to which was attached a piece of dirty, white rag. It was obviously intended for a sign of surrender. But why, Angus asked himself, should the Martians wish to surrender? All three men had evidently suffered rough handling for their clothing was little more than a covering of tatters stained with blood. After a short consultation the two flanking men lifted their empty hands above their heads and all three advanced. Old Jamie hesitated a moment and then unlocked the port, beckoning to them to enter. The questioning he left to Angus who began with the monosyllable:

'Well?'

31

The middle man, looking askance at several pistols trained upon him, lowered his flag of truce and answered with the characteristic lilt:

'We have come to surrender.'

Angus frowned. This was not his idea of Sen-Su's methods.

'And the rest of you?' he asked.

'There are no more.' The Martian spoke slowly and with a depth of dejection.

'Talk sense. There were ninety-seven of you. Where are the rest?'

'All gone. We were attacked. Great winged monsters which screamed fell on us out of the night. We shot at them and then we fought them hand to hand, but it was dark. There must have been thousands of them. We three got separated and they overlooked us or must have thought we were dead.'

'All the rest are dead?'

The Martian shook a sorrowful head as though he considered the indignity greater than death.

'Only a few. The rest they took away. In the fight they seemed flimsy, but their wings are strong. They lifted our men, two to a man, and flew off with them. I don't think they took them far. We came to you because' – he hesitated uncertainly, uncomfortably – 'because you are our kind,' he finished abruptly.

Angus studied him hard, seemed satisfied, and nodded.

'We'll go and see your camp. Maybe we'll learn something there.'

Torrence demurred. 'It's a trap. They knew they couldn't touch us in here, so they're getting us into the open.'

Angus ignored him. The first officer's prestige had fallen to zero with the defeat of his sniping proposition. A dozen men, including old Jamie, set out to investigate.

The Martians had made a clearing for their camp, and when the Earthmen reached it they stopped to gasp aloud. The brown men had excelled themselves. It was the scene of an epic battle. Slaty, grey winged bodies strewed the place – literally hundreds had fallen in that fight. Not only was the ground a bloody shambles of hacked and twisted forms, but in the surrounding trees and bushes hung the corpses of those shot in mid-air. Lanky shapes, somehow unclean, their listless great wings stirring in the gentle breeze like patches of dirty

32

sailcloth, while the steady drip-dripping of their crimson blood incarnadined the leaves below.

For some moments no one spoke. In Joe's mind arose the dim memory of old engravings depicting hell. Then Angus broke the silence.

'What a carnage. I've seen slaughter in my time, but this . . . '

The three Martians went forward and examined the dozen or more bodies of their men lying among those of the grey attackers. The wing talons had made them unpleasant sights.

'Sen-Su?' asked Angus as they returned.

They shook their heads. The leader was not with his dead.

Angus threw back his head and looked speculatively up at the caves in the valley sides. Below one a glimmer of something bright caught his eyes. He pointed it out to Jamie, and the old man brought a pair of binoculars to bear.

'The buckle of a belt,' he said, 'a broad, Martian belt.'

Angus gave the order to return to the ship.

'You're not going after them?' enquired Torrence.

'That's just what we damn well are.'

'But they're enemies and it's our duty –'

Angus stepped close to him.

'See here, you know too doggone much about duty. The Martians are human beings – they're our own kind. What's more, there are our own men to be found, too. If you think I'm going to stand by without reason while men of Earth, or Mars, are in the power of these repulsive spawn of miscegenation, you'd better think again. Get that?'

Torrence wisely withdrew. Old Jamie proved reluctant to let them go, and sternly forbade any of his colonists to take part. He did his best to dissuade Angus though his manner showed that he had little hope of succeeding. Perhaps he spoke from a sense of duty, for when he found that the other was determined, he became lavish in his offers of weapons.

Rifles were discarded as unsuitable, but he insisted that each man should take several pistols since, in the unlikely event of success, the rescued must be armed. He pinned most faith to the long knives which would be invaluable for in-fighting. In addition, he insisted that all the available lamps be collected and affixed to the chests of the rescuers.

The *Red Glory* colonists collected to bid them farewell. There was a suspicion of envy in the eyes of some of the younger men, but Jamie's word remained law.

'Good luck, laddie, and God be with you,' said the old man to Angus.

He watched the twenty-seven from the *Argenta* and their three Martian companions with wistfulness as they scaled the valley wall. That was the spirit which had taken the Earthmen all over the system. Confidence that they could not lose the game. The last figure turned and waved a hand as it disappeared over the skyline. Old Jamie sighed. He wished he were young again, he'd show them – but he wasn't young. He was an old man, and getting sentimental.

He sighed again and turned back into the *Red Glory*.

VI

THE CAPTIVES

David awakened to a species of bedlam. He could hear Angus's shouting voice making a bass accompaniment to an unearthly screeching. He heard the other men jump up from sleep and leap into action. He started up with them, fumbling for the knife in its scabbard by his side. His hand was upon the hilt when long arms wrapped around him, pinning his own arms. He cried out. Dimly he could see furious activity taking place in the cave-mouth; dark shapes which jerked and fought. He struggled against the retaining arms aware only that this was an attack, by whom or what, he could not tell, though his mind jumped to the conclusion that the Martians were somewhere back of it.

He opened his mouth to call again, but before the cry came something was wrapped around his head. A dark sheet of unfamiliar substance which, by its feel, sent a surge of panic through his nerves. He lashed out as far as he could reach with his feet, but a moment later they were snatched from under him and secured by arms which seemed to wrap themselves more firmly about his legs than any human arms could hold. He wriggled, trying vainly to jerk off the grip. Through the shroud about his head he could still hear the sounds of turmoil,

34

but they were swiftly growing fainter, and he could tell from the motions of his captors that he was being carried away.

At length the sounds dropped behind altogether, and the silence of their progress was broken only by soft footfalls and occasional, high pitched cadences from his bearers. He succeeded in twisting his head in the folds which covered it, and began to breathe more easily. With a faint hope, growing even fainter, he strained his ears in hope of pursuit. At last, hope died altogether. Perhaps all his companions had also been captured; perhaps they were dead; he did not know. He was only aware that all hope of rescue had gone.

For seeming hours the steady progress continued. At last his bearers seemed to find their method of transport inconvenient. They halted and set him on his feet. The arms about him remained inexorable, but the stifling cover was removed from his head. Thankfully he drew great breaths of fresh air, but he could see no more than before. The darkness was solid; unrelieved by the faintest glimmer. There came sounds of much movement near at hand. A few shrill notes such as he had heard before, and a grunt which might have come from a human throat. His heart bounded, and he decided to risk the return of the stifling cover.

'Hullo? Who's there?' he asked quietly.

An exclamation of surprise came out of the darkness.

'Cleary here. That's Robbins, isn't it?'

'Anyone else?'

There was no answer.

'I'm sure there were some others,' said the doctor's voice. 'But they're not here now,' he added a little unnecessarily.

'What are these things, and where are we?' said David.

'Lord knows what they are, but we're certainly somewhere inside Asperus.'

The captors continued to ignore their prisoners' talk. After a few minutes' rest they picked them up once more and continued their way through the darkness. This time progress was less uncomfortable, since there was no smothering cover.

'Do you know how many there are?' David enquired.

The doctor did not.

'If we could only see what they're like, I'd feel less uneasy,' he said.

They carried on a conversation in desultory phrases for some time. David had long ceased to struggle, and, as a result,

35

his captor's hold had insensibly loosened. With the utmost caution he pressed his arms a little outward. His hand was already near his knife; with a little more play he might be able to snatch it out.

The ruse began to work. The arms did not tighten with suspicion, but eased a little to rid themselves of the strain. David was beginning to extend his elbows further when the party came to a sudden stop.

From the darkness ahead came the click of something hard against metal, followed by a grating sound. Gates opening, David guessed. A moment later they stopped again and a similar series of sounds denoted another gate. Within a few minutes David began to see the first dim signs of reflected light on the wall where the tunnel turned, many yards ahead. He waited with a quickening excitement until he could see his captors. Two were carrying him, and, by turning his head, he could see two more dealing with the doctor. He took a deep breath and snatched for his knife.

The movement was a complete surprise. The first his bearers knew of it was that the blade was in his hand – it was almost the last they knew, for he cut at them savagely. Their screaming cries were deafening in the enclosed space. The hinder pair rashly dropped the doctor and hastened to their assistance. A second later he, too, was after them, knife in hand. David slashed wildly, dodging their raking claws and their attempts to entangle him in their wings. With the doctor's arrival in a rear attack, the fight was soon over. The two men, panting, faced one another over the four grey bodies.

'We must hide them quickly,' said David. 'Some more are bound to come along after all that row.'

Hastily they dragged the corpses into a small side passage and stood tensely listening. After a little while they relaxed. The grey creatures' cries, whether of alarm, or for help, appeared to have passed unnoticed. The problem now before them was one of direction. The way behind was out of the question, for it was barred by gates, and they faced the alternative of creeping along dark, narrow side passages or risking the lighted area ahead. In the end they elected for the latter; both had had enough of the darkness, and their enemies seemed unhindered by lack of light. The doctor adjusted his glasses which he had miraculously retained intact. He was a small man,

36

inclined to stoutness and showing, in normal conditions, a cheery, rubicund face.

'Yes, towards the light, by all means,' he said.

He was aware of some slight professional regret that they could not spare time to examine the bodies of their late enemies, but he appreciated the necessity of getting clear.

They cautiously turned the corner ahead and found themselves facing a long vista of deserted tunnel lit at intervals by small, glowing lamps in the ceiling. There appeared to be no reason for this transition from darkness to light. David was aware of misgivings. This was the way their captors had been taking them, and it was obviously, for that reason, the way they should not go. However, if they should be attacked, they would have at least the advantage of seeing their attackers.

They walked on, every sense alert and their knives tightly clutched. To keep to the centre of the way seemed safest; one could not tell what might lurk in the small, unlighted side passages. Two hundred yards further they rounded a corner and abruptly debouched upon a still larger tunnel. Should they turn left or right? This new way, as dimly lit as the other, gave no clue. They were able to see perhaps fifty yards in each direction before turns cut off the view. David was about to speak when the doctor checked him. A faint sound had reached him from the left. Both peered in that direction, but its origin remained hidden by the corner. They drew back into the lesser tunnel to wait.

The approaching sound resolved into a steady trudge; the swish-swish of soft slippered feet upon the rock floor. David breathed more easily, for the monotonous walk could not be made by anyone seeking to investigate an alarm. The steps slowly continued to near the end of their passage. A figure which looked neither to left nor right, passed by. Both the watchers stared. They had expected one of the winged creatures, but –

'An Earthman,' gasped David.

The man caught his voice and turned towards them. He was elderly, and his head was but sparsely covered with grey hair. His face was pale and deeply graven with lines, but, for all its sorrow, it was kindly. Strapped upon his back he bore an enormous basket filled with broken ore. His expression changed to amazement as he saw them. He took an involuntary step in their direction and then stopped with doubt in his eyes.

37

His attention seemed fastened more on their clothes than their faces.

'Who – who are you?' he asked in an unsteady voice.

David told him.

'You have come from "Outside"?' Something in his pronunciation of the last word seemed to imply inverted commas.

'We have,' admitted David, watching him closely, 'and we want to know how to get back.'

The old man slowly shook his head. A strange, musing look seemed to come over his face.

'There really is an "Outside"? Sometimes I think it was just all a dream.' He paused, looking at them with unseeing eyes. 'But no,' he added, 'it was no dream. A man could not dream a sight so lovely as a tree with the wind in its leaves, or the glory of the sun, any more than he could dream the curve of a wave.'

David and the doctor glanced at one another. The old man had forgotten their presence. He went on:

'Twenty-five years, oh God. Twenty-five years since I have seen those things.' The last word was a sob, and the tears ran unashamed down his cheeks. David took hold of his arm. He spoke gently.

'You don't understand. We want you to show us how to get out.'

The old man shook his head again.

'My boy, it is you who do not understand. – There is no getting out. Nobody has ever got out.'

'But – '

'Nobody, in twenty-five years.'

At the sight of their puzzled faces, he pulled himself together. The dreamy look vanished from his eyes and he spoke in a different voice.

'Come along with me, I'll explain.'

David relieved him of the basket and fixed it to his own, more able, shoulders. He was surprised to find it much lighter than it appeared, until he remembered the small size of Asperus.

The three walked together along the tunnel, crossed a hall which showed signs of being a natural cavern enlarged, and entered another tunnel. His name, said the old man, was John Fordham, and he began to relate the disastrous history of the *Red Glory*. He had, it appeared, been among the first to be

38

taken prisoner. He was still talking when they reached another rock hall. In it a number of men and women were seated at long tables. All conversation ceased as they entered, and Fordham introduced them to the company:

'Two men from "Outside".'

The same look of suspicion that they had seen in Fordham's eyes appeared now upon every face, but, like his, it began to fade at the sight of the newcomers' clothing, as though their uniforms were assurances of identity. Both men and women present were clad in inadequate garments patched together from many pieces of coarse cloth. David estimated those present at one hundred and fifty, and subsequently found that he was only seventeen short of the actual figure. Most of them were of middle, or later, middle age, with a sprinkling of the really elderly, and a very few younger members of approximately thirty or thirty-one. He noticed at a glance that women predominated.

With the lessening of suspicion they came crowding round, fingering the men's clothing as if it were something rare and precious, and asking innumerable questions. David slipped the basket of ore from his shoulders and dropped it on the floor. At his request for something to eat, bowls of fruit were immediately produced. The two attempted to answer the incessant questions as best they could. They described their own capture, but of conditions aboard the *Red Glory* they knew nothing. They could only say that Angus had sighted a wreck which might, or might not, be the *Red Glory*. At last the spate of questioning eased, and they had a chance to put their own perplexities forward. What were these creatures they called Batrachs? What was happening in this subterranean world? Was there really no possible means of escape?

Dr. Cleary was particularly exercised in the matter of the Batrachs. He had seen enough of them to form the opinion that they were mammals, but he was certain that no such forms had been found elsewhere in the system. He had a theory that similar systems produce similar forms, with, of course, adaptations to heat and gravitation, and he was fond of his theory. The presence of the Batrachs shook it severely.

Nobody was able to enlighten him. It was, it appeared, a subject never discussed with the Batrachs.

'You talk to them?' asked David incredulously.

'But of course – or, rather, they talk to us for we can imitate

39

only a very few of their sounds. To get anything out of us, some of them had to learn our speech.'

'They're not savages then?'

'Depends what you mean by a "savage". The Batrachs are highly intelligent in their own way, if that's what you want to know.'

'And your position is – ?'

VII

'WE'RE SLAVES – NOTHING MORE, NOR LESS'

David frowned in a puzzled fashion. He had just been told that the Batrachs numbered hundreds of thousands, if not millions. Surely it was not worth their while to enslave so few Earthmen. Several thousand slaves would have been understandable, but to maintain this handful of men and women couldn't even be economic. Ever since capture they had been confined beyond the double gates and all their food must be brought down from the surface. Their work could scarcely pay for the labour of feeding them. He put the point to Fordham who attempted to explain.

'As we told you, the Batrachs are intelligent, but their intelligence is difficult for them to apply. Perhaps you will find it easier to understand if I compare them with ourselves. Now, the first stepping stone of man's climb from savagery is really his opposed thumb. Don't misunderstand me, I know that there were lesser factors, and I don't forget that apes also have opposed thumbs, but the fact remains that without that useful tool, it is more than doubtful whether man could ever have risen as he has.

'Early man picked things up and played with them. He found in time, for instance, that if one stone were placed upon another, he could by standing on it, reach a fruit otherwise out of reach. He did not think the action out first; he did it by accident, and then took advantage of it. Once it had been done, his intelligence was stirred, and he could do it again. You see, this is the important point, his hands taught his mind in the beginning. The reasoning mind did not take real control until far later. If you doubt this, just consider how lazy people still try to make their hands teach their minds; they do it whenever they apply what we call a "hit and miss" method. So much for contrast.

'The Batrachs' intelligence, however, is fundamentally different. Their minds have not grown from actions. Somehow their mental evolution has progressed without the promptings of physical organs. The result is that they have reached a sticking point and they realise it. They can think, but they cannot *do*. They have no opposed thumb to help them. Control of their limbs is coarse compared with precision bequeathed to us by thousands of generations. Their talons have no more capability of fine accuracy than the claws of a tiger. They were – and are – in fact, in a very similar position to a paralysed man. Their only method of getting things done is to cause others to do them. And we,' he ended bitterly, 'have been those others.'

Cleary sat for some time in thought before he asked: 'But this vast system of caves? They're artificial. If your theory is right, they couldn't have dug them.'

'They might. It requires no great accuracy, and if you look you will see that all the work is rough and unmathematical in finish. But I suspect that there have been other captives before us. There are the gates. They are very old. Then, too, they have a few metal instruments – crude, of course, but certainly not made by the Batrachs themselves.'

The doctor went on to ask more questions. The suggestion of the Batrachs' curious development interested him considerably. David's attention lapsed by degrees. He found his gaze wandering first over the rocky walls and bare utilities of this cave, which he understood, was the main living-room of these lost Earthlings. From this he fell to examining the faces of those about him: tried to imagine what twenty-five years in such surroundings would mean, and failed. A sudden thought struck him. All these men and women had lived together for a quarter of a century . . .

'Are there no children?' he asked.

Even as the words left his lips, he realised that they were an indiscretion. A cold silence greeted the question. No one attempted an answer, and the eyes of all refused to meet his own. He had committed a dire solecism – touched a subject under strict taboo. It was queer – the condition of at least three

41

of the women . . . He turned a bewildered face to the doctor. The little man shrugged his shoulders ever so tightly. Tactfully, he asked another question of John Fordham, and the awkward moment passed, though not without leaving a vestige of constraint.

Conversation was terminated by the sudden ringing of a bell. All present turned to face one of the tunnel mouths expectantly. After a wait of a few seconds, a figure strode out of it into the hall. Both men from the *Argenta* stared in surprise. They had expected the grey form of a Batrach, but the newcomer was a tall, well-built, young Earthman. His face, though clean cut, was pale and there was a sense of familiarity about it which David was at a loss to understand.

The men and women respectfully drew back, leaving a clear space down which he marched without a sideways glance until he reached a small, desk-like table at the head of the cavern. At it he seated himself to face the gathering, and in a hard, emotionless voice began to recite the names of those present. They had leisure to examine him more closely.

His age was around twenty-three, and he had the air of a man who performed a distasteful duty conscientiously. His clothing consisted of a knee-length tunic below which appeared trousers. Both garments were embroidered with patterns of geometrical design, as were the soft sandals on his feet. The roll-call completed, he paused a moment, then:

'John Fordham,' he said curtly.

The old man stepped forward. In a flash David saw the reason for the elusive familiarity of the young man's face. It was a youthful edition of the older man's. His son, perhaps? But there was no filial feeling in the curt voice.

'John Fordham, you have been reported to me as being one basket of iron ore short today. Why is this?'

The basket still lay where David had dropped it. As he made a movement to pick it up, the young man noticed him for the first time.

'Who are you?' There was the slightest flicker of surprise in his eyes as he scrutinised the pair. David hesitated and then explained, carefully omitting reference to the deaths of their captors.

'From "Outside"?'

Curious, David thought, this manner of treating the simple

42

word 'outside'. The present emphasis on it was very different from the old man's.

'Yes,' he said.

'There has been a mistake. You should not have been brought here. You will follow me.'

They hesitated, but David's neighbour whispered:

'Go with him. He will take you through the gates and you will have a chance then. You've still got your knives.'

The young man took good care that his body should screen the combinations of the double gates as he worked them. The two with him noticed that they were leaving by a different route, for the tunnel was lighted and sloped steeply upwards.

In the walk of half a mile which followed, Cleary tried their guide with a number of questions which did not raise the success of even a monosyllabic reply. It was noticeable, also, that when they approached closely to him, the young man drew away with some ostentation. At length they began to meet or overtake others; men and women who had occasion to use one or other of the many side turnings. These, too, drew close to the walls as they passed, and more than once they saw noses wrinkled in distaste. The tunnel brought them at length to a hall.

The place was comparable in size with the cave in which the *Red Glory* survivors dwelt, but it was better lit, and better furnished. It even showed attempts at decoration by strictly geometric forms. But the greatest difference was that it was filled with the cheerful sounds of laughter and young voices. David felt a lightening of the load of depression which had crept over him. The doctor continued to wear a frown on his round face.

To complete the contrast with that other cave was the fact that every man or woman in sight was young, and many small children ran or crawled upon the floor, romping as freely and happily as any child born on Earth.

A pale cherub of four was playing near the entrance. David smiled at him and extended a friendly hand. The child looked up at the sound of his voice. One glance was enough; he gave a frightened howl and ran to bury his face in the tunic of a young woman nearby. The look David received from her dark eyes was murderous and loathing. She hastened away, comforting the frightened child.

43

David turned to the doctor in amazement. He felt slightly resentful; children, as a rule, liked him.

'What is it? What's wrong here?'

Cleary, still frowning, refused to commit himself.

'I don't know yet, but I've got an idea – just the glimmer of an idea.'

Their guide led out across the hall. As they approached the people shrank back to either side, the children ran whimpering to the women. Not a face in all the place, but expressed disgust. Twice they had to pause before groups which had not noticed their coming. Each time the young man called: 'Outside', and the way cleared as though by magic. A queer fancy floated into David's mind – were not lepers in the East compelled to call 'Unclean' with much the same result?

They left the hall behind and still continued upward through the labyrinth. Now and then they had occasional sights of the grey forms of Batrachs going about their unknown business. Mostly they were on foot, but in the larger tunnels it was possible for them to fly, passing over the Earthmen with great swishes of their dry wings. The lighting grew dimmer as they proceeded and soon it became necessary for the guide to produce a lamp.

David began to toy with the idea of snatching the lamp and making a break for freedom. Surely, after all this climbing, they could not be far from the surface. He nudged Cleary and pointed suggestively to his knife. For some reason of his own the other shook his head. David let the matter drop and a few moments later, when the rays of the lamp fell upon another gate, was glad he had. It was opened like the others by a combination lock. The young man stood back for them to pass. The click of its fastening followed – but the man with the lamp was on the other side. Too late David realised what had happened. This was not another gate along the way, it was the door of a prison – and they, like fools, had walked straight into it. He drew his knife and sprang back, but the young man was safely out of reach. He turned away, paying no attention to David's threats, and soon his lamp became no more than a receding glow in the distance.

Darkness, intense and almost palpable, closed in. David shook the barred gate in futile fury, but he stopped abruptly at the sound of a movement in the blackness behind him.

44

'Who's there?' Mentally he cursed his voice for its unsteadiness; this dark was bad for a man's nerves.

A voice replied with a familiar, lilting tone.

'Good God, the Martians!' he cried.

VIII

ANGUS INVADES

Angus paused to muster his party at the cave-mouth.

'No talking!' he ordered, 'and step as lightly as possible. The brutes are nocturnal, and it's odds on we'll catch them sleeping now. Come on!'

He switched on the lamp upon his chest and led the way into the mountain. The entrance cave was much like the one in which they had been attacked. The dry, dusty floor sloped down towards the beginning of a narrower tunnel in which they could not walk more than two abreast.

They wound for fully half a mile of its evenly descending length before they came to the first forking of the way. Joe guessed that already they were below the level of the valley outside. Angus stopped and turned an investigating beam up each of the facing tunnels. Both were similar in size and in the degree of use they showed. One of the men picked out a slight obstruction on the smooth floor of the right hand path. He jumped forward and returned, displaying his find.

'A Martian boot,' said Angus, handling the soft leather. 'Somebody in that gang knows his stuff. Let's hope he's managed some more clues.'

The hope was fulfilled. They were subsequently assured that they were on the right track first by the discovery of the fellow boot, and, later, by the sight of a discarded cap. As yet they had had no sight of the Batrachs, and still the passages led down. Twice Joe, bringing up the rear, thought he heard a dry rustle behind him, but each time he swung his lamp, it revealed only the empty tunnel. They had now penetrated a long way into Asperus, and his suspicions were aroused.

'This is too easy to last,' he told himself uneasily.

45

A few minutes later, his fears were borne out. An unmistakable, murmurous swishing came from behind him. And, this time, the lamp showed a solid phalanx of grey, winged forms sweeping down in a rear attack. Almost without thought he drew his pistol and sent half a dozen shots crashing among them. Not a bullet could miss. They hesitated as several of their number fell, and swayed indecisively for a second. They rallied and came on, but their advance now was slow and deliberate. They appeared to have abandoned the notion of coming to grips.

Angus continued to lead his men steadily forward. Retreat was, for the present, cut off, but that had been almost inevitable in such catacombs. There was more pressing business to be attended to before they had to worry about the way back. Joe reloaded his pistol and held it ready.

A turn of the passage brought them without warning into a large cave. The many black tunnel entrances dotting the walls on all sides suggested that it was a meeting place, a kind of public square of this subterranean world. By far its most disturbing feature was that in almost every entrance lurked grey, menacing figures. Angus grasped the danger at once. The Batrachs would have full room to use their wings and could attack from all sides simultaneously. Already not a few were taking to the air. The way behind was blocked. A swift glance showed that the tunnel directly opposite held no guard, and, at his command, the Earthmen made for it, crossing the wide floor in a series of leaps. To their surprise they reached it unattacked. The sense of uneasiness grew. The Batrachs followed at a distance.

'Don't like this,' muttered Angus. 'From what we've seen of them, they're fighters. I'll bet anything the blasted creatures have got something up their sleeves.'

Nevertheless, they continued unmolested for several hundred yards. Then, at a corner, Angus stopped dead. The way ahead was choked with Batrachs who stood blinking in the glare of the lights.

'Oho! So that's it. Sandwiching us, are they?' He settled a pistol in one hand and a knife in the other. 'Now for it!'

But still the Batrachs did not attack. There was a puzzled pause. Angus opened his mouth to speak, but before a word came, the floor gave way beneath him.

The next seconds were confusion. A writhing mass of men

46

fell struggling sideways, swearing as they tried to disentangle themselves. Angus's pistol was knocked from his hand by the fall, but he staggered to his feet, still clutching the knife. The light on his chest remained unbroken, but it was obscured by the struggling bodies. The man next to him suddenly grabbed his arm. Angus tottered and lost his balance. He tripped over a prostrate form, and slid, head first, down a polished stone slope at prodigious speed. After a few breathtaking moments he sped from a kind of chute into a room crammed with the grey Batrachs.

The trap had been well planned. Half a dozen of them flung themselves upon him before he could rise. His knife arm was pinned to his side and despite all the extra power which the low gravitation gave him, he could not break their tenacious holds. Struggling and shrouded beneath the great wings, he could see little, but he was aware that others of his band were suffering a similar fate as they shot into the room. He could hear their muffled curses and grunts as they fought.

With a colossal heave he achieved a sitting position and struggled thence to his feet. The Batrachs still clung about him, pinioning his arms. By jerky, intermittent beams he could see all over the floor a series of struggling heaps with wings threshing furiously above as the men were secured and weighted down by numbers. He tried with all the force of desperation to wrench his right arm free, and bellowed futilely at his assailants:

'You lot of lousy sons of Satan. Just you wait till I get this knife free – I'll show you who's boss here. I'll carve your miserable stringy carcasses into mincemeat, you –'

But the thin arms twined around him like ropes; not an inch did they give before all his violence. In the far corner he glimpsed Joe Seely rise for a moment, only to be dragged desperately down. The outlook was becoming ugly.

An interruption occurred. A grey curtain on the opposite wall – made, he suspected from wing membrane – was twitched aside. In the doorway behind stood the short figure of Sen-Su. The Martian's clothes had been torn away, and the blood streamed down his brown skin from a dozen ragged cuts. In one hand he held a jagged ended metal bar. His expression was one of dismay until he saw Angus, upright, though helpless. His bullet head went down. He crouched, whirling the bar before him like a lethal flail, and launched forward in a mighty leap at the group which held the engineer. His crude weapon tore through the great wings as though they had been rotten cloth.

The Batrachs' thin bones snapped like sticks as his blows went home. The onslaught was more than they could stand; the hold on Angus loosened. They and others with them flung themselves upon the threshing demon, smothering him in their wings, twisting their long arms about him to bring him, still fighting, to the ground.

But Angus broke free. His long knife darted with a shimmer like lightning, slashing, thrusting, tearing about him. Those whom the blade touched sank to the floor; those whom it did not, backed from his neighbourhood. Chaos broke loose. The Batrachs holding other prisoners were trodden under the feet of their own kind in flight before Angus. Their grips slipped and the prone men snatched for their knives. Within a few seconds there were five at Angus's side, driving the grey ranks headlong with a line of slicing steel. The din of piercing cries increased as more and more men rose until all were on their feet. The surviving Batrachs fought each other to escape through the narrow doorway. A bellow of rage came from Angus. One of the escaping horde had hooked his sharp wing talon in the flesh of Sen-Su's shoulder and was dragging him away. Angus leapt in and slashed; slashed once and the wing was severed; slashed again and the head rolled away. He picked up Sen-Su and carried him aside. The Martian smiled faintly at his rescuer, then, swiftly, his expression changed. He pointed through the doorway.

'The others,' he cried. 'Quickly, before they get them away.'

Leaving a half dozen men to guard the few Batrach prisoners, Angus and the rest sped down the corridor. From somewhere ahead came the shrill sounds of Batrachs mingled with the confused babble of human voices. The next turn revealed winged figures fumbling frantically at the locks of barred gates set in side walls. They twisted around and emitted high cries as they saw the running men. One glance was enough to assure them that safety lay in flight. With mournful shrieks they disappeared into the blackness ahead.

A pistol made short work of the locks on the cell gates.

As the imprisoned Martians filed out, Angus caught sight of two familiar, lighter faces.

48

'David, Cleary,' he called. He greeted them excitedly and at once dragged the doctor off to have a look at Sen-Su's wounds.

'He's game,' he said. 'If he hadn't managed to break out of his cell and take a bit of the bars with him, we'd all be in cells by now.'

'Where are the rest?' he asked David as Cleary made his examination.

David looked puzzled.

'I mean the six men who were taken when you were.'

It was the first David had heard of them, and he said as much. Angus frowned.

'Then we'll have to go on – we can't leave the poor devils here.'

'There are more than those six,' said David. He told briefly of the *Red Glory* survivors and the others they had seen on the lower levels. Angus's frown grew still deeper as he listened. It was not a pleasant thought that Earthmen and women were existing here as slaves. He was at something of a loss to know how to proceed. Not only would it be difficult to find the way into these further tunnels, but there was no telling what further tricks the Batrachs might have in store.

'See if you can get anything out of the prisoners,' David suggested at length. 'They might be – er – persuaded to talk.'

Angus stared.

'You mean that they can talk? Those things?'

'I was told that some of them can – it's worth trying.'

One of the prisoners readily admitted to a knowledge of English. Was, in fact, fluent from long association with the slaves. His extremely high-pitched voice had a fraying effect on the nerves and he met with difficulties in the forms of labials, nevertheless, he was intelligible.

His information caused Angus to make a complete reassortment of ideas. Hitherto, he had considered the Batrachs as he would a species of wild animal – intelligent animals up to a point, but undisciplined; governed by no other instinct than that of the herd. But the view he was now given of them as a race under central authority, pulling together towards an ideal, killed all his preconceptions stone dead. He began to see, for instance, that the piles of dead on the site of the Martian camp represented not stupid ferocity, but determination and sacrifice. The Batrachs did not go into battle from sheer fighting instinct, but with a clear knowledge that many of their kind must fall for the eventual good of the race.

As one of his theories after another was tumbled down, it became clearer that he must take an entirely different course. He began to think of them as Bat-men, no longer as animals, a mental attitude which was the harder to adopt since hitherto no forms of life in the whole system had even competed intelligently with man. But there was one idea which underwent no readjustment – the Batrachs, whatever their status, must not be allowed to keep Earthmen and women as slaves.

Angus considered deeply.

With the rescued Martians and David and the doctor they numbered now one hundred and eight. Not a nugatory party, but certainly not formidable. In addition there was some shortage of arms and several men had been badly mauled. In continued skirmishes with groups of Batrachs their resistance would soon be worn down. Clearly a policy of guerilla warfare was unsuitable. He turned back to the prisoner.

'You talked about government. What form of government is this?'

Apparently there was an official council. The Batrach began to explain with some pride how it was formed. Angus cut him short.

'Take us to this council,' he ordered.

The Batrach agreed with an alacrity which caused him secret misgivings. He did his best to shake them off. After all, as he pointed out to David, whatever happened, it could scarcely make their position any worse.

IX

BEFORE THE COUNCIL

The Council Chamber, to which their guide led them, proved to be a cave of medium size, but sufficiently large to contain all the party. Word of their coming evidently preceded them, for they found a row of the creatures waiting; fifteen grey Batrachs who watched their arrival with calm, interested eyes. They sat upon a kind of stone shelf, seven to each side of one who was raised a little higher. It worried Angus a little that they showed no trace of fear, nor even anxiety, but, without delay, he plunged into the heart of the matter, addressing the central figure.

'We understand that you are holding a number of men and women of Earth prisoners here?'

The other studied Angus unhurriedly. When he answered, it was in a voice of lower pitch than their prisoner's, but still unpleasantly shrill.

'We are,' he said briefly.

'And we demand that you free them at once.'

'You "demand"?' The Batrach showed a tinge of surprise at the choice of words. David and Joe exchanged glances. Both would have favoured a less outspoken policy. The party was scarcely in a position to 'demand' anything. But Angus merely nodded.

The Batrach forbore to point out that they were virtually prisoners themselves. He asked:

'And why do you think we would surrender prisoners to you who are useful to us?'

'Because you would stand a very poor chance of success against a warship from Earth.'

The Batrach considered.

'But if we imprison you, Earth may never know.'

There was an uneasy stir among most of the Martians and Earthmen present, but Angus smiled.

'That,' he said triumphantly, 'is where you are mistaken. You have held the passengers from the *Red Glory* only because we did not know what had become of them. We thought that the ship had been destroyed. Had we even suspected the true state of affairs, you would have had a visit from a warship long ago.

'Now, however, the case is altered. The *Argenta* is un-damaged. If we fail to return, someone will take her back to Earth and report. Should you manage to prevent this, the delay will only be slight for our destination was known to officials at home and they will shortly send out a searching party.'

His words evidently went home to the council. They started to speak in their shrill, wailing tones. The central Batrach quieted them.

'It would mean the end for many of us,' he admitted, 'but I doubt even your people's power to conquer and hold all our

51

passages and caves. It would, in fact, be better for them not to try. We could trap party after party so that they would starve. We know your weapons and we know their limitations.'

Angus shook his head.

'You know only a few of our weapons.' He went on to describe in some detail the effects of some poison gases, and to tell how the heavier types could be poured into the tunnel mouths to percolate throughout the Batrach warrens and kill any who got so much as a sniff of them.

Dissension followed. A few of the Batrachs took his statement for a fairy tale, others who had heard of gases from the slaves, knew better.

'But the prisoners – your own people – they would die too,' one objected.

Angus drew himself up.

'It is better,' he bluffed, 'for an Earthman to be dead than to be a slave. Our men would not wish to kill their own kind, but they would do it sooner than know that they lingered in servitude.'

He watched anxiously to see how this piece of heroics would be received. If it failed, he must change his tactics entirely. During the discussion which followed he kept his gaze level and steadfast. At length the spokesman addressed him again.

'We will agree to your demands. The survivors from the *Red Glory* shall go free.'

Angus allowed himself to relax slightly, but before he could reply, David was whispering in his ear.

'The others,' he was saying, 'the younger ones. Don't forget them.'

At the suggestion that these also were included in his demand, a great screeching of objections arose from the council. Again the spokesman quieted the rest with a wave of his winged arm.

'They are the children and the grandchildren of the others,' he said. 'We call them the New Generations. They have never been on the surface. They know only these caves which are their homes – it would not be kind to them to take them with you.'

Angus and his party stared. 'Would not be kind?' The effrontery of it. Would not be kind to take them into the sunlight – out of this gloomy labyrinth. He grew angry and

52

his demands became eloquent. The Batrach listened patiently with a look in his eyes almost as though he were secretly amused. Once he began to break in with an objection. Angus swept on, brushing it aside unheard. At last he stopped. The spokesman, still with the disconcerting light in his eyes, hesitated and then gave in.

'We will agree not to stand in the way of their going,' he allowed.

Angus had won, but he was not easy. In the middle of his victory he was aware of a twinge of that same misgiving he had experienced earlier in the passages. Again it seemed too simple, and there was a something in the Batrach's tone.

The mixed party of Earthmen and Martians was conducted to a large cave to await the coming of the slaves. A few were jubilant and confident. Man, in their estimation, had triumphed again, as man always would. But the majority was alert. Like Angus they felt that all was not so cut and dried as it appeared. There was a sense if not of treachery, at least of something very like it, in the air.

A group comprising Angus, David, Joe, Torrence, the doctor and Sen-Su – the latter bandaged, but not seriously hurt – stood apart from the rest, discussing the possibilities of the situation in undertones. Torrence was emphatically of the opinion that the Batrachs were not fetching the prisoners, but mustering for a mass attack with the intention of wiping out all in the cave.

Angus did not agree. For one thing he trusted the chief Batrach's word, and, for another, his threats of invasion from Earth had made a deep impression. All speculation was cut short by the arrival of a party of persons at the near end of the cave. One look showed David the people with whom he had recently talked.

'The *Red Glory* survivors,' he said.

The pitiful procession came slowly towards them. John Fordham walked a little ahead of the rest. There was no joy in his bearing; his feelings seemed too deep for that. He approached them, shuffling and tired, his shoulders bent as though they still supported his basket of ore. He looked at them with eyes which seemed to doubt what they saw. His voice quivered and broke as he asked:

'Is it true, what they told us? Are we really going "Outside"?'

'Yes,' Angus told him gently. 'It's quite true. We're taking you home.'

'Home.' The old man stood quite still. His arms hung slackly by his sides. His head went back as though he gazed beyond the rock about him, beyond the millions of miles of space, towards a swinging planet which was home. His breath caught in his throat. He buried his face in his hands and wept.

A woman came to David and plucked at his sleeve.

'And the children?' she asked in a low tone. 'The New Generation?'

'They're coming too,' he assured her.

She received the answer in silence. Drew a breath as though to speak. Shrugged her shoulders hopelessly and turned from him to join the others. There was no joy in her manner as she imparted the news. David almost followed her to ask questions, but remembered in time how his last question of the kind had been treated. He decided to wait for this puzzle to solve itself.

Up the far end of the cave another disturbance was occurring and he turned in company with the rest to discover that the New Generations were entering. Exclamations of surprise broke from both Earthmen and Martians as the stream of young men and women and children filed in. Nobody had thought to consider the probable number of the children and children's children.

Angus had guessed at a possible hundred or so. Suddenly confronted with more than five hundred, he stared with widening eyes. Even David and the doctor though somewhat prepared were taken aback. Cleary indulged in some hurried mental arithmetic.

The newcomers, accompanied by several Batrachs, remained crowded together at the end of the cave. Most kept their gazes averted, though a few examined Angus and his party with a kind of furtive interest. Their communal attitude was one of puzzled indecision. A short discussion resulted in one man detaching himself. As he approached, David recognised the firm step and fine carriage of their late guide. At a distance of two yards from the group he stopped short, scanning them with a look of distaste. He spoke in the tone of one accustomed to lead.

'You are from "Outside"?'

Again that curious treatment of the final word.

'We are,' Angus replied.

'What do you want here?'

Angus's eyebrows rose. This was scarcely the expected attitude of rescued towards rescuers.

'We have come to set you free.'

'Free?' The young man was puzzled. 'I don't understand you. We are free.'

There was a puzzled silence. Angus supplemented:

'We have a ship on which to take you, and your parents, back to your native planet – Earth.'

The young man continued to look mystified for a while. Then a thought appeared to strike him. With a look of growing, indignant horror in his eyes he asked:

'You want us to go "Outside"?'

'Of course,' said Angus curtly. He did not care for the young man's expression.

There was a muttering among the listening crowd of the New Generation. Partly nervous, but in greater part indignant. They shrank back towards the tunnel through which they had entered.

'Look,' whispered the doctor to David, pointing towards the group of original survivors. Most of the women were starting towards the New Generations with a complex expression. David analysed it as mingled yearning and hopelessness. He became aware that the groups of emotions in all parts of that cave fitted with none of his expectations.

'What is it?' he whispered back. 'I'm all at sea.'

Cleary shook his head.

'I think I'm getting it, but I'm not sure yet.'

Meanwhile, on the young man's face, anger replaced consternation.

'How dare you make such a suggestion?' he demanded. 'No doubt you think that by those – ' he pointed at Angus's weapons ' – that you can force us. It may surprise you to know that you underrate us – we are not cowards. Get back to your filth. Get back to your "Outside". I am ashamed that our women have been allowed here to hear such an infamous, indecent suggestion. Had I known that they were to be exposed

55

to such ignominy as this I would – '

Angus stepped forward, eyes narrowed. The young man recoiled; not from fear, but as though he avoided contamination. He turned round, addressing the crowd of the New Generation, already moving to the tunnel.

'Go!' he shouted. 'Go before the evil from outside can touch you.'

He wheeled back to Angus. His countenance was a study in abhorrence, but he stood his ground, warding off the other from his people. Angus advanced slowly, bewildered. He put out his hand to press the other aside. The young man gave a cry of disgust, tore off the garment Angus had touched as though it were unclean, and hurled it from him. A loathsome reptile might have inspired the look which now dwelt in his eyes. A quick glance showed him that the last of his people were leaving. Without another word he turned and strode after them.

The silence of consternation held the cave. One voice rose at last to break it; John Fordham's.

'My son,' he cried. 'My son.'

But the retreating figure marched into the tunnel with never a backward glance.

x

THE POWER OF THE BATRACHS

Angus broke his trance of astonishment. Several of the *Red Glory* women had begun to sob desolately, hopelessly. He called Sen-Su to his side. Looking into his eyes he said:

'Sen-Su, can we work together?'

The Martian smiled slightly.

'Because I asked that question, they condemned me to exile. My whole faith has been that men should work together instead of exploiting one another.'

'And so they shall, by the Lord. We Earthmen have been a pack of fools – you've convinced me of that, Sen-Su. Henceforth, I'm with you Martians. When we get back to Earth – '

'But now we are still on Asperus,' Sen-Su pointed out. 'What do you wish me to do?'

'I want you to tell some of your men to take these *Red Glory* people to the surface, and to the ship. I'll send some of mine along too, to explain to old Jamie that it's on the level. Will they do that?'

Sen-Su nodded and turned to address his men in lilting Martian. A number of them crossed over and posted themselves beside the rescued.

'And the rest of us?' he enquired, turning back.

'The rest of us are going to get the New Generations out of this warren, whether they like it or not,' snapped Angus.

'You'll never do it,' Cleary prophesied quietly.

Angus glared.

'Who says?'

'I do. You don't know what you're up against.'

'I know that these damned Batrachs are holding them somehow.'

'I doubt it; I don't believe that the Batrachs could persuade them to go. They've been clever; they've hit mankind in his weakest spot. Damned clever.'

Angus shrugged his shoulders and went about directing the departure of the rest. The survivors at length trailed away, a weary, dejected lot. Some seemed half afraid to leave their prison. Twenty-five years is a long time, and their children had refused to go . . .

As the last of them disappeared a company of grey forms flew out of a large tunnel and up the cave. Angus's hand flew to his knife and then dropped as he recognised the Batrachs of the Council. The creatures alighted a few yards away and closed their wings. The leader advanced.

'They would not go?' he asked Angus.

'You knew damn well they wouldn't go. What I want to know is, why wouldn't they go? How did you stop them?'

'We did not stop them. They could have gone had they wished.'

'You did not hypnotise them? They were free?'

This time the Batrach really smiled.

'Freedom. How often have I heard the slaves speak of it? — It is the obsession of your race. What is freedom?'

It occurred to Angus that this was not the simple question it sounded. He wrestled with it awkwardly:

'The power to do as you want.'

'Then the New Generations are indeed free.'

Angus gave it up. 'I don't believe you,' he said bluntly.

'Nevertheless, it is true. If you took the New Generations away by force – as perhaps you might – you would take them from happiness to misery.'

'I don't believe that, either. How can they be happy down here in these burrows?'

'You don't appreciate your own point. "Freedom is the power to do as you want." – Has it not occurred to you that the "want" might be suggested?'

Angus frowned. Someone else had spoken of suggestion. Yes, Sen-Su had referred to it as one of the great forces. He looked at the Martian and saw comprehension dawning in his eyes.

'Come,' said the Batrach. 'Words won't convince you. I must show you why the New Generations will stay.'

He turned and led the way up an ascending passage. As he went he talked, giving them what was in effect an amplification of Fordham's explanation to David. The Batrachs, he reiterated, were making a great bid for the future of their race. They had knowledge, but they could not make even so simple a thing as a book to store that knowledge for the benefit of future generations. The Batrach held up his clumsy wing claw. What, he asked them, could be accomplished with so crude an instrument as that? They had tried always to educate the claw, but it was little use compared with even an uneducated hand with the advantage of the power to grip. They had been forced to turn to other methods.

'Just so, I am told,' he said, 'did your ancestors turn to the horse and to other animals to overcome some of their own limitations. Did you ever think of your horses as slaves?'

Doctor Cleary diverted the subject with a question.

'How did you Batrachs get here – there are no others that we know of in the system?'

'I can't tell you that,' the other admitted. 'There are legends, but they are vague. They tell of the Mother of all Batrachs, so great, so magnificent in her wings, that she could fly not merely as we fly, but out to the furthest stars in the sky. Now and again, however, even she tired and needed to rest, and on each world where she rested, she brought forth ten small Batrachs such as we. You can make what you like of that. It may be that the Mother was in reality, a space ship such as

58

yours. I do not know. One thing is certain, and that is that we are admirably adapted to Asperus. We should be unable to fly on even the smallest of the major planets.'

'There is usually a basis of truth in such legends,' agreed the doctor. He was determined to protect as long as possible his theory of systematic species. He went on to question the other on his physical structure.

The rest of the men followed in silence as the two conversed. David and Joe felt little more than a curious interest in what the Batrach would reveal. Angus wore a puzzled frown. Torrence, as usual, was out of temper. He had abandoned the making of suggestions, but he knew what a man's attitude should be towards an inferior race. This meeting on an equal footing was, to him, not only improper, but weak. Sen-Su was paying close attention to the leading Batrach's talk, while the rest of the Council seemed to be content to bring up the rear.

At last came the glimmer of daylight far ahead. The Batrach led on without a pause. The doctor, watching him closely, saw that his eyes filmed over with a protective membrane as the light grew more intense. The passage rapidly broadened out until it became a wide cave with an extensive view over valleys and crags. On the rocky floor twenty or more children were playing with simple toys. In careful attendance lurked the figures of tall, grey, female Batrachs. Evidently this was the nursery of the grandchildren of the *Red Glory* survivors. David, mindful of his earlier experience, hung back, but Angus continued. A child noticed his coming and fled with a yelp of terror in the direction of the nearest Batrach. There was an indignant murmur from Torrence that the children were being taught to hate their own kind. He was surprised when the leader calmly nodded:

'But only those from "Outside",' the latter added.

'I don't see – 'Angus began.

The Batrach checked him. 'Watch,' he said.

He indicated a small boy who was near the cave mouth. Outside, the sunlight was pouring down on a broad, smooth ledge. The contrasting world beyond seemed to intrigue the youngster. He was slowly edging towards the fascinating line of light. Once he looked back cautiously towards the other children and their attendants, but they gave no sign of noticing his manoeuvres. He crawled on to within six inches of the line of shadow and hesitated again. Finally he made up his mind and boldly stepped over. There was a sudden, earsplitting crash from a metal gong. A breath of nauseating stench seemed to invade the cave. The child jumped back howling with terror. One of the female Batrachs swept forward and picked him up in a fold of her wing. He hid his face with its streaming tears in the comforting darkness it afforded.

'Behaviourism,' cried the doctor. 'A pure Behaviourist method.'

Angus's eyes were blazing with anger. He advanced upon the Batrach as though he would strike him.

'It's cruelty,' he shouted. 'Pure, wanton torture of these children. I see it all now. You've brought up the New Generations to be so scared of you that they daren't do a thing you might resent. You had only to tell them that you wished them to stay, and they cringingly obeyed.'

Cleary intervened. 'Don't be a fool man. Did the leader, old Fordham's son cringe? Of course he didn't. He walked like a ruler. Besides, these children don't hate the Batrachs. Look there.'

The female Batrach, in a motherly way, had dispelled all the child's terror. He was clinging to her and almost laughing again. Angus and the others stared in bewilderment. There was no cruelty in the soft eyes with which she looked at the child – only concern that it should be happy once more. Torrence, in the background, muttered vengeful threats.

'I'm damned if I get this,' Angus said. 'First she allows the child to be terrified out of its wits – then she's really worried when it is. What's it all for?'

'It's on the Behaviourist basis,' said the doctor, enthusiastically. 'A matter of conditioned reflexes.'

'That's all Greek to me.'

'You know what a reflex action is?'

'One that is instinctive.'

'Not quite that. One that takes place without conscious thought – not quite the same thing. An instinctive reaction is innate, but a reflex action is caused by subconscious memory.'

'That seems pretty much the same.'

'No, it's not. Take our avoidance of fire. Very young children are attracted by the brightness of fire. They want to play with it – have no instinct to fear it. But you and I do not try to handle fire, in fact, we avoid coming into contact with it.

But we don't say to ourselves each time, "This is fire – I must avoid it." The warning is subconscious – we "automatically" avoid it. In other words, sometime in the past we burned ourselves and stored up the subconscious memory that fire was painful.

'A conditioned reflex arose – it caused us to avoid anything in a condition of fire. It was the same with foods; some we "automatically" leave alone because we know they will make us ill. The same with all kinds of things. As a result we dislike even the smell or taste of them. Once you cut yourself on a sharp knife – now you "automatically" pick a knife up by the handle.'

'Then this . . . ?' asked Angus, indicating the children.

'All the children here will grow up hating the world outside, and that hatred, properly fostered will become an inhibition. They will not be able to leave these caves. The memory of that gong and the nauseating smell won't remain conscious for long, but, if the treatment is continued (as, no doubt it is) the idea that "Outside" must be avoided will persist. From the behaviour of the adults it would appear most successful.'

'Do you mean to tell me that if I, as a child, had been treated in this way, I should hate the "Outside"?' demanded Angus.

'Certainly – why should you be different?'

'But – but I'm free. I can think for myself.'

'You think you can – but can you really? Every thought of yours is based on somebody's teaching, or a scrap of information picked up from somebody else. One might even say that there is no "you" – you are no more than a conglomeration of bits of other people. It's true,' he added as Angus shook his head, 'think it over a bit. You are as much a product of conditions as these children will be.

'Given a completely uninstructed child, a blank canvas, so to speak, there is scarcely any code of belief, morals or behaviour which cannot be induced by careful training. You've only got to look at the violently differing codes upon Earth to see that.

'That's what the Batrach meant when he asked you what was freedom. We are always prompted or guided by others whether we like it, or not. Sen-Su said that suggestion was all powerful. He was right. This is its most subtle application.'

THE ALTAR

There was a pause while all the men regarded the children in silence. The idea was slowly sinking into Angus's reluctant mind. Was it possible, he was wondering, to warp minds so that they saw nothing but horror in the fresh greenness of trees; so that the sun ceased to be the life giver, but became something indecent and fearful, never to be looked upon? It seemed impossible, and yet...

David, too, was thinking. He remembered the decorations in the caves of the New Generations – not a natural form had been allowed to intrude. Every suggestion of the world 'Outside' had been rigidly excluded. He remembered, too, the expressions he had faced – hate, fear and disgust . . .

Torrence was not thinking. This foolery was taxing both his patience and his control. It was no mean task to keep his tongue still.

Again a child was approaching the line of sunlight. They watched in silence an exact repetition of the earlier episode.

'But why the gong?' asked Joe. 'Why not stop them each time?'

'That is simple,' the Batrach explained. 'Were we to stop them, they would resent it and end by disliking us – as it is, we comfort them after their fright and they love us for it.'

Joe's mouth opened wide. He had never considered the possibility of anyone loving a Batrach.

'Come,' the tall, grey figure added. 'I will show you one more piece of the life of the New Generations. I think it will convince you.'

He led the way back into the tunnel. The doctor hurried forward and walked abreast with him.

'Then you do not mind the *Red Glory* survivors leaving?' he asked.

'No. We could only get the coarsest of compulsory labour from them. It was their children we wanted. We had, at first,' he added, 'some difficulty in persuading them to bear.'

He went on to explain. The survivors' children had been taken from their parents as soon as possible and started on an elaborate course of conditioning to environment. Success had been immediate and the New Generation had been brought up thinking, feeling, acting and reacting in the ways the Batrachs wished – yet unaware of any compulsion. When the second generation began to appear it could be safely left with its parents save for regular periods of training in a nursery such as they had seen. The change was really very slight, he pointed out, none of the basic instincts was touched and character remained unaltered – only certain taboos became desirable, and certain desirables, taboo.

The doctor nodded thoughtfully.

'And so,' he said, 'our strongest point is our weakest.'

The Batrach was puzzled.

'I mean, our adaptability. It is that power which takes us into dry climates and wet tropics and polar regions, cold planets and hot planets, open spaces and confined quarters – has, in fact taken us all over the system. You have succeeded in turning that same adaptability to your own advantage.

'The others do not understand how the New Generations can be really happy in here, but I do. There never was (in this system, at least) a race so adaptable as we.'

The Batrach checked at last at a small doorway. Making a sign for silence, he led the way within.

They emerged upon a shelf partway up the wall of a large cavern. In the arrangement of the place there was more than a suggestion of the interior of a church. Row upon row the New Generations sat below them all gazing intently towards the far end at a feature which caused the Earthmen to stiffen with surprise. A long table stretched right across the cave and was covered by a cloth decorated with metal thread. The ornaments which rested upon it gave it the appearance of a kind of altar. Behind, outspread so that they covered most of the end wall, was a pair of wings patterned after those of the Batrachs. They had been skilfully fashioned from grey, lustrous metal which gleamed under an ingenious arrangement of the dim lights. Below them a man dressed in a grey tunic was in the act of mounting a few steps which led to a kind of rostrum.

He reached the platform and stood for a moment with his back to the audience gazing up at the great wings above him. Then he turned and began to speak in a calm, clear voice. His pale face was serious and there was no doubting the sincerity and strength of the belief which backed his words. But what words they were . . . The men's eyes grew wide as they listened.

' – Our ancestors sinned. They doubted, and doubt is sin. For that sin they were punished. They were cast into the nethermost "Outside" – a place of evil and terrors without names. They forfeited all; they had betrayed their faith and, as a punishment, their wings' – he dropped his voice as though grieving – 'were withered upon them. Shorter and shorter grew their arms, and less, generation by generation, the spread of their wings until, at last, the membrane was gone and they were left as we are with but stunted growths.'

In a gesture he held out a pair of magnificent arms and stared at them.

'These,' he stretched them out towards the audience, 'these are the symbols of our fall; the badge of our shame.

'But' – his voice rose triumphantly – 'through faith we shall win back. Beyond hope – damned through all eternity – are those "Outside". But our feet are already upon the road back. The Batrachs have taken us in and purified us. Here in the caverns of the chosen they have taken compassion upon us. We shall climb again to that high estate from which our ancestors fell.

'Slowly and surely we shall rise, scaling the firm rungs of faith. It will not come in our time, nor even in our children's time, for the return to grace is hard, but far, far in the future, men who have regained their lost wings – such wings as the Batrachs have – will look back upon us and praise us for our faith which paved the way. Therefore, I tell you, keep faith. Firm, steady and unfaltering faith so that a million yet to be born may one day look back and honour you. Imagine a man in the full glory of his restored wings who will whisper the name of one of you, saying: "She was my mother, and faith, my cradle." '

As the last words died away he turned to face again the huge, symbolic wings upon the wall. He raised his arms imploringly and stood motionless. There was not a sound to be heard in the cave.

On the ledge the men stood speechless, astounded by the travesty. There had been no bluffing. They caught the spirit of the men and women below. Intense, faithful, trusting, and, above all, convinced. That the Batrachs had taught this religion and the worship of the Wing, there could be no doubt – but that it had become a part of the worshippers' lives, there was equally little doubt. So simple.

A slightly new twist to the old Earth legend of angels, and there was the ideal, with the Batrachs already in the position of demi-gods.

David remembered old John Fordham's words – 'The Batrachs can think, but they cannot *do*.' He had been right. They had thought a new race of mankind into being, and this race, regarding them as saviours, would work for them willingly and joyfully, secure in their faith. David's last hope died; the New Generations could never be rescued against such odds.

Torrence broke the silence with a shout. He swung himself over the edge of the rock shelf and dropped to the floor below. Before any could stop him he was on his feet and racing towards the far end. He leapt upon the rostrum and felled the speaker with a blow.

'Fools!' he shouted, swinging round on the startled audience. 'Fools! He lied to you. Nothing but lies. It's a plot of the Batrachs. Men never had wings – they never will have wings. They –'

'Blasphemer,' roared a voice. An echoing pandemonium broke loose, drowning Torrence's voice with its babel.

The audience rose to its feet. With murder in its eyes, it charged madly towards the rostrum.

Angus knew an infuriated mob when he saw one.

'My God, they'll lynch him,' he cried.

The Batrach beside him swooped down from the ledge and spread his wings; another followed his lead. Together they sped towards the lone figure of Torrence, at bay beneath the monstrous metal wings. Their talons snatched him up and lifted his struggling figure clear of the crowd just in time. A moment later they brought him back, pale and not a little scared, to the ledge. The Batrach, after a glance at the outraged worshippers on the floor below, led the way into the corridor. There, he turned and looked at them with eyes which held the faintest tinge of mockery.

'You are convinced?'

Angus nodded unhappily.

'You're devils, but you're clever devils.'

'And you will leave us in peace?'

'What else can we do?' Angus shrugged.

'You might gas us,' observed the Batrach with an inflection which called the bluff.

'All right. You win,' admitted Angus miserably.

'Goodbye,' said the Batrach.

As they took an uphill tunnel, Angus turned to the doctor.

'And you really think they're happy here?' he asked.

'Less unhappy than they'd be anywhere else,' was the reply, 'and what more can you wish any man?'

Sen-Su's lilting Martian voice joined in:

'And now?'

'And now,' responded Angus, 'we go back to Earth to preach the brotherhood of man and the damnation of Batrachs.'

And so, though it is colonised, you will fail to find the word 'Asperus' on Earth's proud colonial lists.

No Place Like Earth

The decision was difficult – remain at peace on Mars, or migrate to Venus and rebuild Earth's lost heritage. The outcome would be momentous.

(The sequel to 'Time to Rest'.)

On the left bank lay the ruins of a great city. According to the Martians it was called something like Thalkia. It was unlike any waterside city, unlike, indeed, any city that Bert had seen on Earth. There were no vestiges or signs of quays. Instead, half a dozen stone-paved roads, ramps with low walls ran from the land into the water. Looking over the side of the boat one could follow them down into the murky depths. From them Bert had deduced that the Great Ones who had built the city had employed some kind of amphibious craft, able to run from the canal into the market-places or wherever it was that the cargoes were needed. It was just another of those hints about the Great Ones that, put together, added up to practically nothing.

Several times Bert had stopped there, and made his way among the ruins. They told him little: he could not deduce even the size or nature of the Great Ones. Pale red sand had crept across much of the place. Out of it protruded pillars and walls of the darker red stone, and between them the corners of fallen blocks. Here and there great lintels, architecturally fantastic, and structurally impossible on Earth, still stood. It could be seen that the Great Ones had abhorred the straight line, delighted in the subtle curve, and had had a particular penchant for a gently swelled three-sided pillar. And, too, that there was nothing ephemeral in their building notions. Allowing for the different gravity, there was a massiveness which nothing on Earth, save possibly the Egyptian pyramids, had employed. It awed Bert quite a deal to be standing in the remains of the oldest structural work anyone had ever seen. The civilisation of Earth seemed by contrast like a quickly blown and burst bubble. He doubted whether Thalkia had looked much different at the time when men's ancestors were leaving the trees for the ground. Each time he had come away humbled by antiquity, and with the desire to dig there one day and find out more about the Great Ones.

Yet this time as his boat chugged past Thalkia he almost failed to notice the place. His arm was over the tiller, and he steered without thinking. The eyes under his battered hat's brim were not even conscious of what they saw.

Many miles behind him, beside a smaller canal than this, stood a ruined tower that had changed from its obscure original purpose to become the home of a Martian family, and it was there that his mind was lingering. The family sustained itself on the produce of a few fields irrigated by the usual wheel beside the canal. It was to keep the wheel turning and to repair such domestic objects as confounded the limited local talent that Bert had the family on his schedule of calls. Of seven Martian years (which would have been something over 13 Earth years had the disintegrated Earth survived as a measure of time) Bert had spent more than six wandering the canals in his boat, leading a tinker's life from which he returned occasionally to base at the Settlement to pick up metal, make a few pots, and collect such supplies as he could conveniently remove. The small farms and scarce villages on his route had become used to him, and to putting broken objects aside for him to mend when he called, and he had grown to know and to like the people who lived in them. At first, to his Earth-raised mind, they had been too quiet, and ineffective, and fragile-looking, so that like most of the Earthmen he had thought them decadent. But in time he began to see himself and the other Earthmen with something like Martian eyes – as neurotic, acquisitive, and with values which were sometimes suspect. He had begun to wonder whether 'drive' was always the virtue he had been taught it was – whether it might not sometimes be the expression of instability or poor integration. Though that was not a thought one would mention to another Earthman.

'To us it seems,' a Martian had once told him, 'that a sense of guilt lies on each of you Earthmen. You all of you think that

68

you ought to be better men, or bigger men, or at least different men in some way. We wonder why a whole race should have the inferiority complex which makes it base its virtues on the assumption of its own inadequacy. To us that seems strange.'

It seemed strange to Bert, too, and not very palatable when put in that way, so that he had disputed it. Nevertheless, as time went by, he had found himself understanding Martian views better, and Earthmen's views less well.

It was disagreeable to realise, too, that the Martians mattered more now, for the Earthmen were finished. The 'drive' of the Earthmen, which was something superimposed upon the normal will to live, had brought them to the end. By accident, carelessness or irresponsibility it had torn the Earth into the millions of fragments which now circled the Sun as an inner asteroid belt. The few hundreds of men left stranded here and there were of no account any longer. It made little difference whether they died off from drink or illness, or waited for old age to take them. In less than thirty Martian years the last of them would have gone, and the brief disturbance of their incursion would gradually drop out of Martian memory, leaving no sign but some admixture in the Martian blood – Which brought Bert back to considering the family that lived in the ruined tower.

There, as in other places, he had been accustomed to tell tales to the children as he worked. He had been only half aware that they were growing up. Mars was a world so spent, so far into old age, that younger generations still growing up there seemed not only incongruous, but pointless to an extent where he scarcely admitted to himself that they were doing so. His last visit, however, had left no doubt about it, for the youngest daughter, Zaylo, whom he thought of as a little girl, had suddenly become transformed into a young woman. The realisation had disquieted him in a way that was quite new . . .

Bert had come to some sort of terms with the conditions thrust upon him. He was not interested in the few Martian girls who hung around the Settlement. Occasionally he came across one of the Earthmen who had settled down with a Martian girl. Sometimes it seemed a qualified success, more often it didn't. In the early days some such idea had tentatively entered his own head, but he had dismissed it, rather as he had dismissed the idea of an alcohol-soaked life in the Settlement. The indications were, he decided, that it did not work well.

Bert was not analytical in the matter. It had not occurred to him that the chief factor in a Martian marriage would be the temperament of the man concerned – his ability, or lack of it, to adapt. Nor had he looked closely at the motives of his decision. He was aware that he resisted something, but had anyone told him that in his heart he was sentimentally preserving a useless loyalty to a world and a race that had finished, he would not have believed it. If his informant had gone further, and told him that the Earth he revered was an idealistic, romantic conception with little likeness to the vanished Earth of reality, he would not have understood.

What he did understand was that the sight of Zaylo had somehow pulverised in a moment a philosophy which had hitherto been adequate enough, and that the placidity of his existence had been torn to shreds. In his mind he could hear the voice of Annika, Zaylo's mother, saying: 'Life is not something which you can stop just because you don't like it.' He did not want to believe that. There had been a poet once who wrote:

> I am the Master of my Fate,
> I am the Captain of my Soul.

That was what Bert believed – or hoped.

Ever since the day when he had accepted the grim fact that he was stranded on Mars for the rest of his life he had steered his own course. He had shown the Greater Fate that it could not get him down, and he intended to go on showing it. Zaylo was a trap – a beautiful trap, like a fly-eating orchid. The sight of her and the sound of her voice had pierced through all his defences. He ached from the resulting wound. He knew perfectly well that if he were to stay near her he could no longer hold that Captaincy undisputed. He was jealous of her power to move him, angry with her for revealing to him the dry sawdust within his life. – And so he had run away . . .

He was now in the process of discovering the paradox that it takes a very strong mind to run away really efficiently, and that if the mind is that strong it probably doesn't run at all. Certainly he had been unsuccessful in his efforts to leave Zaylo behind. She stood between him and everything.

When his eyes were on the massive ruins of Thalkia, what he was seeing was Zaylo. Zaylo in a deep yellow skirt stencilled with a pattern in warm brown, with her hair held high on her head by three silver pins; the delicacy of her hands and arms, the unhidden beauty of her young breasts, the curve of her shoulder, her skin like copper woven into satin, dark eyes looking depthlessly back into his own, red lips trembling on a smile . . .

But he did not want to see Zaylo. Deliberately he banished her. 'Those,' he told himself aloud, 'are the ruins of Thalkia, one of the greatest cities of Mars. That means only five or six miles now to Farga's place. Take the waterway forty-five degrees right at the junction. Let's see. Farga . . . ' He consulted his notebook to refresh his memory regarding Farga's family and household. Farga's son, Clinff, would be pretty well grown up now. A useful boy, more mechanically minded than . . . And then somehow he was thinking of Zaylo who was also pretty well grown up now. He was watching her moving with the grace of a young Diana on delicate feet that seemed to caress the ground, noticing the carriage of her head, the rhythm of her walk, the –

Bert shifted, and muttered. He brought a determined gaze to the water ahead. Yes, Clinff had a better mechanical sense than most of them. One might be able to teach him . . . It was queer how difficult it was for Martians to grasp the simplest mechanical principles. Take the lever. When he had tried to explain it to Zaylo there had been a delightfully earnest little furrow between her brows . . .

Farga walked down to meet him as he ran the prow ashore on the shelving bank. The Martian was smiling and holding out his hand in welcome – it was a custom which he had picked up, and punctiliously observed with Earthmen. Bert had a first impression that he was slightly surprised by the visit, but in their greeting he forgot it. He slung a sack of belongings and tools over one shoulder. Farga laid hold of a smaller bag, but failed to lift it. Bert reached down one hand, and raised it easily. The Martian shook his head, with a smile.

'On the moons of Jupiter I, too, would be a strong man,' he observed.

'If I could go back to Earth now, I guess I'd be as weak as a kitten,' Bert said.

'As a what?' enquired Farga.

71

'As a – a bannikuk,' Bert amended.

Farga grinned broadly. 'You – a bannikuk!' he said.

They ascended the bank and made their way through the fringe of clinking tinkerbells which crowned it.

Bert was glad, and a little surprised, to see that Farga's house was still standing. After Farga himself had built the walls of flat, uncemented stones, Bert had selected suitable roofing slabs from the Thalkian ruins and ferried them down. When he hoisted them into place he had doubted the strength of the walls to support them, but Farga had been satisfied, so they had left it. Even after years on Mars Bert still found his judgments of weight and strength fallacious; Farga was probably right, and the structure had no weather to contend with, only heat and cold.

The place was the ordinary pattern of Martian homestead. A few fields strung along the canal bank, a wheel to irrigate them, and the house – which was part shed and granary, and part human habitation. Meulo, Farga's wife, appeared in the doorway of the dwelling part as they approached. Other interested but much smaller faces showed at the mouths of burrows close to the house, then the bannikuks came scampering out, filled with their usual insatiable curiosity. They began to climb Bert's trousers the moment he stopped. He discouraged them gently.

The inside of the house was clean. The floor was paved with a jigsaw of flat stones. There was an immovable stone table, its top polished by use; a set of stools carved from soft rock. In one corner stood a simple loom – an object of some value for several parts of it were wood – and in another was the bed with a mattress of dried, strawlike stalks. No one could say that Martians were sybaritic. On the table Meulo had set out a dish of what the Earthmen called potapples, for they looked like potatoes, and tasted, with the help of imagination, very slightly like apples.

Bert dropped his burdens and sat down. Four bannikuks immediately raced up the table sides to gather in an interested group immediately in front of him. Meulo shooed them off. Bert picked up a potapple, and bit into it.

'Things going well?' he enquired.

He knew what the answer would be. A farmer's living on Mars was sparse, but not hazardous. No vagaries of weather, few pests. Trouble usually arose through the few simple tools wearing out and breaking. Farga recited a brief list of minor calamities. Meulo added one or two more. Bert nodded.

'And Clinff?' he asked. 'Where's he?'

Farga grinned. 'You know what he is – interested in machines, almost like an Earthman. Nothing would hold him when he heard the news. He had to go off and see the ship for himself.'

Bert stopped in mid-munch.

'Ship!' he repeated. 'Ship on the canal?'

'No – no. The rocket-ship.' Farga looked at him curiously. 'Haven't you heard?'

'You mean they've got one to work again?' Bert asked.

From what he recalled of the dozen or so ships lying on the Settlement landing-ground it did not seem likely. The engineers had early reported that all the remaining fuel if pooled would leave little margin over one take-off and one landing – so no one had bothered. Perhaps someone had succeeded in making a satisfactory fuel. If so, they must have been mighty quick about it, for there had been no talk of any such thing when he had left the Settlement half a Martian year ago. And why try, anyway? There was no Earth to get back to. Then he recalled that during the first years there had been a number of rocket rumours which turned out to have nothing in them. The Martian grapevine wasn't any more reliable than other bush-telegraphs.

'When was this supposed to be?' he asked cautiously.

'Three days ago,' Farga told him. 'It passed south of here, quite low. Yatan who is a friend of Clinff's came and told him about it, and they went off together.'

Bert considered. All but three of the ships at the Settlement had been stripped or broken up. The three had been kept intact because – well, someday, somehow there might be a use for them that nobody really believed in.

'Which ship was it? Did he see her name or number?'

'Yes, she was low enough. Yatan said it was a long name in Earth letters – yours, not Russian – and then A4.'

Bert stared at him.

'I don't believe that. He must have made a mistake.'

'I don't think so. He said it was different from all the ships at the Settlement. Shorter and wider. That is why Clinff and he have gone to see it.'

73

Bert sat quite still, looking back at Farga without seeing him. His hand began to tremble. He did his best to control his excitement. A4 would, he knew, be one of the new atomic-drive ships – at least, they had been new thirteen Earth-years ago. There had been a few in more or less experimental service then. Everybody had said that in a few more years they would replace the liquid fuel ships entirely. But there had not been one of them among those stranded on Mars. Perhaps the boy had been right . . . What he had said about the shape would be true. Bert could remember how squat they had looked in pictures compared with the lines of normal space-ships. He got to his feet unsteadily.

'I must go to the Settlement. I must find out,' he said, speaking as though to himself.

Meulo made as if to protest, but her husband stopped her with a movement of his hand. Bert did not notice either. His eyes seemed to be focused on something far away. He started towards the door as if in a dream. Farga said:

'You're leaving your tools.'

Bert looked round vaguely.

'My – ? Oh, yes – yes.'

Still without seeming to know what he did, he picked them up.

They watched him go, with the bannikuks scampering unnoticed round his feet. He trudged on, brushing through the tinkerbells, setting a thousand little leaves clinking and chiming as he passed, and disappeared over the rim of the bank. Presently came the familiar sound of his boat's engine, then it speeded up, greatly beyond its usual phut-phut. Farga put his arm round Meulo.

'I feel I ought not to have told him. What can there be for any of these Earthmen? Their world has gone. Nothing can bring it back to them,' he murmured.

'Someone else would have told him,' she said.

'Yes – but then I should not have had to be the one to see such loneliness suddenly in a man's face – and such empty hope,' he told her.

When the night made its sudden fall Bert switched on his light, and kept travelling. For the first time he wished that he had built his boat for more speed. On the third night he fell asleep at the tiller and grounded on the gradual bank with just enough impact to awaken himself to his need of proper sleep. On the fifth day he reached the Settlement.

In all that journey Zaylo troubled only his dreams. When he was awake his thoughts continually brought back pictures of Earth – That was stupid, he knew. Wherever the rocket had come from, it certainly could not have come from the swarm of circling asteroids which now represented Earth. Yet the association of ideas was unavoidable. It was as if an old locked box in his mind had been opened, letting scenes and reminiscences spring out as the lid was raised. And he made no honest attempt to force them back.

For the last few miles he might have been upon an ocean. The body of water formed by the junction of several important canals, the curvature of Mars, and his own lowly position took him out of sight of land. But presently he was able to make out the slender spire of the useless radio mast dead ahead. An hour or so more, and he had driven the boat ashore at her usual berth. He jumped out, drove the grapple into the sand to hold her there, and strode off towards the Settlement.

The moment he set foot inside the fence he was aware that the place felt different. On previous visits its spiritlessness had closed around him like a blanket that became a little thicker each time. But now that sensation was missing. The few men he saw on his way to the central clubhouse did not drift in the old way. They looked as if they had received an injection which made them walk with a purpose.

In the clubhouse bar-room the transformation was a little less complete. A number of the habitués sat at their usual tables, too alcohol-logged and sunk in cynicism to change much. When he had helped himself to a drink he looked round for someone who might be coherent and informative. A group of three talking earnestly at a table by the window caught his eye. He recognised the two bearded men as out-of-Settlement men like himself. He crossed the floor to join them. The man who was doing most of the talking was pale and sallow beside the others, but he had the more decisive manner. As Bert came up he was saying:

'You put your names down now, that's my advice. I'm willing to bet you get chosen for the first batch – You, too,' he added, glancing round as Bert pulled up a chair. 'We want men like you. Half of them here have gone rotten. They'd never pass any physical examination – or stand the change. I'll put your names up right now, if you like – with a priority mark to 'em. Then once the doc's looked you over, you'll be all set. How about it?'

The two agreed without hesitation. The man wrote down their names, and glanced interrogatively at Bert.

'I'm only just in. What's it all about?' Bert asked with an effect of calmness. He was rather pleased with the way he was managing to control the excitement thumping in his chest. 'All I've heard is that a ship is said to have come in,' he added.

'It's here now,' said one of the bearded men.

'From Venus,' added the other.

The pale man talked. The other two listened as eagerly as if all he said was fresh to them too. There was a gleam in their eyes and a look of purpose on their faces. Bert had not seen a look like that for a very long time.

'Ever been to Venus?' asked the pale man.

Bert shook his head.

'The trip here was my first,' he said.

'There's a future on Venus. There's none here,' the pale man told him. 'Things are going ahead there. We'd have let you know that long ago, but for that static layer over the place that cuts the radio out.'

He went on to explain that it had been clear from the time of the first landings there that Venus could be given a future.

'Here on Mars,' he said, 'conditions were far better than any-one had expected. The atmosphere was a great deal denser and higher in oxygen content than anyone had estimated, and the temperatures more tolerable. It had been thought that only lichens or similar low forms of life could exist. Well, we were wrong about that. All the same, it is pretty nearly finished here now – well on the way out. There are the useful deposits of minerals which for some reason the Great Ones never bothered to work, but that's about all. It had gone too far to be worth a serious attempt to colonise. As for the moons of Jupiter – well, anybody who's content to spend his whole life in a heated space-suit might live there, but no one else. But Venus was something different . . .'

In a rather elementary manner he went on to explain why Venus was different. How the conditions on the younger planet could be considered as approximating roughly – very roughly

– to those on Earth some millions of years ago. How the density of the atmosphere helped to offset the increased heat of the Sun so that, though the tropics were impossible, conditions at the poles were tolerable if not comfortable. How, in fact, it was possible to consider colonisation of limited areas.

'And we were still doing that – just thinking about it, that is. We had got as far as establishing an exploring and shipping base on the island of Melos not far from the northern pole, when we found out more or less by chance that the Slavs had sent out two loads of emigrants and actually established a colony on an island near the south pole.'

'I never heard of that,' Bert put in.

'You weren't meant to. The Slavs kept quiet about it. They were kind of pathologically prone to secrecy, anyway. We kept quiet because we didn't want a first-class international row on our hands. We'd have had to do something about it – and we knew that if we started we'd be in for some full-scale nastiness. The best thing we could do seemed to be to start our own colony, pronto.

'Well, the Slavs had the drop on us there. They'd done a bit of criminal transportation on simple, old-fashioned lines – the way we used to do ourselves. But nowadays we had to get recruits for it. That wasn't easy. Maybe you'll remember a lot of blarney on pioneer lines. Bands, flags, receptions and all that? A lot fell for it. But there had to be other incentives, too, and as decent conditions as we could manage when they got there – And in that we did score over the Slavs. They'd just sent their lot out with as much equipment as they thought strictly necessary – and it's wonderful how little that can be in a tough, well-ordered state. But then, the Slavs are a tough people.

'Still, with all the start we could give 'em our first lot weren't stuck on the place – but they'd signed for a minimum of five Earth years, and a pension at the end of it. There were twenty-five families in that first lot. Another twenty-five families were in space on their way there when whatever it was that happened at home did happen.'

Bert nodded. 'I remember. They were due for take-off about a week after we left.'

'They made it, too. Several other ships came in, as well. But a good many just vanished. They tell me that two ships that were on the Venus to Earth run managed to divert here. They hadn't a chance to turn back, of course. Deceleration and acceleration again would have left them with no fuel for landing. The most they could risk was expending some fuel on making the diversion.

'But that didn't apply to an atomic-drive ship. The *Rutherford* A4 had left Venus two days before, and she did have the reserve of power necessary for a stop, start and land, so she got back – with not a lot to spare. As far as we know, the other atomic ships all bought it. A1 was smashed in a crash on Jupiter, you remember. A2, 3 and 5 are thought to have been on or near Earth when it happened.

'So you see our position was a lot different from yours here. We had about the same number of space-port personnel, but we didn't have a whole flock of miners and prospectors – just a few explorers, botanists, chemists, and the like. And we had a colony containing some fifty women, and nearly a hundred children. Also we had a planet with its best years yet to come. We've got something to work with and to work for. This time the human race has got hold of a planet where it really is in on the ground floor. But what we need right now is as many men as we can get to help us. We'd be getting along a lot faster if we had more to oversee the work.'

'Oversee? What, one another?' said Bert.

'No. We've got the griffas working for us.'

'I thought –'

'You thought griffas were only good for making fur-coats? That's what everyone thought. On account of the price the furs brought nobody bothered to get nearer to them than shooting range. But that's not so. They've got quite enough intelligence to do useful work, and they can be trained up to more tricky stuff when we've got the time. Of course, they're small, but there's any amount of them. The thing is they've got to be watched all the time. There has to be a man in charge – and there's our chief limitation.'

'So what you're offering is a kind of foreman job?'

'That's about it – to begin with. But there's opportunity. It's a place that's going to grow. One day it's going to grow mighty big, and have all that Earth ever had.

'Maybe the climate's not too good, but there are decent houses to live in, and already there's getting to be something that looks like civilisation. You'll be surprised. Here on Mars there's

78

nothing to do but rot. So how about it?'

'You took a long time finding out you needed us,' Bert said.

'No, we knew that all right from the start. Trouble was the getting to get here. That took time. Fuel. To fuel a rocket you've got to produce fuel on the big scale. It takes a lot of labour and time that we couldn't afford for the returns. Just building the plant was too expensive for us to think of. But when we ran across fissile material we could spare the time refining that to get the A4 into use. We want radioactive material anyway, so it became worth doing.

'Now we can take forty-five men this trip, picking the fittest first. You'll make it, easy. You've not let yourself go to seed like most. So how about putting your name down?'

'I'll think about it,' Bert said.

All the other three stared at him.

'God almighty!' said the pale man. 'A chance that's almost a miracle to get off this sandheap – and you'll *think* about it!'

'I was twenty-one when I came here,' Bert said. 'Now I'm thirty-four, Earth reckoning. You kind of grow into a place in that time. I'll let you know.'

He walked off, conscious of their eyes following him. Without noticing where he was going, he found himself back at the canal bank. He sat down there among the tinkerbells and stared across the water.

What he was seeing again was a ruined tower beside another canal. A life that went on there placidly, harmoniously. A group of people content to live simply, to enjoy what life offered without striving restlessly for some undefined end. People who were quite satisfied to be part of a process, who did not perpetually itch to master and control all around them. It was true that Mars was close to dying. But the whole solar system, the whole universe was in the process of dying. Was there really so much more virtue in battling for thousands of years to subdue a planet than in living for a few centuries in quiet content? What was it the Earthmen imagined they sought with all their strife, drive, and noise? Not one of them could tell you that ultimate purpose. For all one knew there was none, it might be just a nervous tic. All their boasts need not be more than the rationalisations of a dominating egoism imposed upon a kind of transcendant monkey inquisitiveness . . .

The Martians were not like that. They did not see themselves as arbiters, as men to be made gods. But simply as a part of life.

Some lines from a poem came into his mind. Whitman had been speaking of animals, but it seemed to Bert to apply very well to Martians:

> *They do not sweat and whine about their condition,*
> *They do not lie awake in the dark and weep for their sins,*
> *They do not make me sick discussing their duty to God,*
> *Not one is dissatisfied – not one is demented with the*
> *mania of owning things...*

The image of Zaylo stepped into his thought's sight. About her like an aura was a sense of peace to soothe his mind and heart.

'Time to rest, Earthman,' her mother had said.

But he had fled because to rest, to settle down, to make a home there seemed like a betrayal of all that the vanished Earth had taught him. The art of surrender to Mars at last, against which the voice inside him still protested: 'I *am* the Captain of my Fate.'

And now there was the chance to join others who thought that way. A pitiful few, but determined to rise again above the catastrophe which had all but finished them.

A vision of Earth as it had been replaced Zaylo in Bert's mind. Cities full of life, wide farmlands rich in crops, the music of great orchestras, the voices of crowds, the liners on the seas and the liners in the air. The world made fit for man by man – the glorious dream of the composite mind of man come true. None who were living now would ever see Earth's genius on its pinnacle again. But it *could* climb there in time. The spirit still was there. One day there would be re-created on Venus everything that had seemed lost with Earth – perhaps it would be a creation even more magnificent.

What he was being offered was a chance to help to raise civilisation again out of disaster. That, or to stay on in puny futility on Mars ...

The image of Zaylo stood before him again, lovely, gentle, like balm for a bruised spirit, like heaven for a lonely soul ...

But there beside her shimmered the spires and towers of new cities springing into Venusian skies, great ships cleaving Venusian seas, myriads of people laughing, loving, living, in a world that he had helped to build.

Bert groaned aloud.

The echo of a puritan ancestor said: 'The hard way must be right: the easy way must be wrong.'

The murmur of another mocked it: 'The way of vanity must be wrong: the way of simplicity must be right.'

No help there.

Bert sat staring into the water.

A sound came from the Settlement behind him. He did not hear it start. He was suddenly aware that men's voices were singing. Occasional drunken bawling was familiar, but men singing lustily, cheerfully, with hope in their hearts was a thing he had not heard for a very long time. He raised his head, listening:

> 'Oh! There's lots of gold so I've been told
> On the banks of the Sacramento...'

It floated across the sands like an anthem. Shades of the forty-niners, ghosts of covered wagon trains crawling, crawling across prairies and deserts, over mountains, foraging on against hardships and hunger. With not much gold at the end, perhaps – only an arid land. But a land which their sons would make to bloom like a garden there beside the Pacific...

Bert stood up. Decision poured into his blood like strong drink. He felt a glow of comradeship for the men who sang. He turned, squaring his shoulders. He carried himself like a man refreshed as he strode towards the Settlement again. Throwing back his head, he let it go with the rest:

> 'Oh-h-h! There's lots of gold so I've been told
> On the banks of the Sacramento...'

Bert was gazing out of the window as the narrow-gauge electric train pulled away. The perpetual clouds which allowed never a glimpse of the sun, hung greyly over the landscape. The grass-like growth on the cleared ground looked pale, insipid, and scarcely green at all. The forest beyond rose like a woven wall of much the same ghostly tint. The details of the distance were blurred, of course, for it was raining – the way it did nine-tenths of the time on Venus.

On one side the line ran close to the landing-field. Hulks of space-ships lay about there like half-flensed whales. They had been gutted of all useful instruments and parts long ago, and huge slices had been cut from the sides of many to supply the need for hard metals. Only the small *Rutherford*, A4, stood intact and shipshape, ready to take off in a day or two on a second trip to Mars. Figures were still busy around her. It was reckoned that she would be able to make three trips during this conjunction, after that she would have to lay off for a while until the next.

Over on the far side of the landing-field coils of black smoke poured from the metal mills and rolled away across country, sooting the pale trees.

Whatever else you might feel about it, you had to admit that a staggering amount of work had been put into the place in thirteen years.

Through the other windows which faced the inner side of the curve the line was taking one could see the houses of the Settlement dotted about. Here and there among them magnificent pennant-trees had been deliberately left standing. Their immensely long leaves rippled in the wind, writhing like Medusa's hair. Crowning the central rise of the Settlement stood the massive pallisades of the seraglio. The upper part of the stockaded wall bristled with down-pointing stakes, and above a top fringed with sharp spines an occasional roof ridge showed.

Bert's neighbour noticed the direction of his gaze.

'Pie in the sky,' he observed, shortly. 'Jam tomorrow.'

Bert turned his head to look at him. He saw a man of middle height, perhaps ten years older than himself. As with all the Venusian colonists his skin was pale, and had a softened, flabby look.

'Meaning?' Bert enquired.

'Just that,' said the man. 'The old dangling carrot. You're one of the lot from Mars, aren't you?'

Bert admitted it. The man went on:

'And you think that one day they'll say: "Okay, you've been a good boy!" and let you into that place?'

'I've been examined,' Bert told him. 'They've immunised me against everything anybody ever heard of, and they've given me a certificate which says I'm healthy and fit for parenthood.'

'Sure, sure,' said the man. 'We've all got 'em. Don't mean a thing.'

'But it certifies –'

'I know – And what'd you have done if it didn't certify? You'd have raised hell. Well, they don't want guys raising hell around here, so they give you one. S'easy.'

'Oh,' said Bert.

'Sure. And now they've given you a job so that you can show you're a good, reliable type. If they're satisfied with your work you'll be granted full citizen rights. That's fine. Only you'll find that they can't quite make up their minds about you on this job – so they'll give you another, maybe one or two more before they do. And then, if you're very, very good and respectful you'll become a citizen – if you aren't, you can still go on trying to make the grade. Take it from me, it's a nice tidy kind of racket, pal.'

'But if I do become a citizen?' asked Bert.

'If you do, they'll congratulate you. Pat you on the back. Tell you you're a swell guy, worthy to become one of the fathers of the new Venusian nation. The old carrot again, pal. Unfortunately, they'll say, unfortunately there isn't a wife available for you just at the moment. So you'll not be able to set up house in the seraglio for a little while. So sorry. But if you go on being a good boy – So you do. After a while you get restive, and go to them again. They're sorry, but nothing doing just yet. In fact there's a bit of a list ahead of you. Trouble is boys took to the climate here better than girls. Very unfortunate just at present. But it'll be better later on. All you have to do is be patient – and go on being good – for a few years, and the balance will right itself. Then you'll be able to move into nice comfortable married quarters in the seraglio . . . You'll have a sweet little wife, become the father of a family, and a Founder of the State. Jam tomorrow, pal . . . If you should get sore, and tell 'em a few things, you lose your citizenship – like me. If you get to be a real nuisance around the place – well, you sort of disappear.'

'You mean that all they tell you is phoney?' asked Bert.

'Phoney, pal? It stinks. Chris Davey took this place over the day after we heard about Earth cracking up. Since then he's let his buddies run it the way they like – so long as they produce the goods. The result is plenty of work for everyone – and no muscling in.'

Bert looked out of the window again. The Settlement was behind them now. The cleared ground on either side of the line was planted with unfamiliar, almost colourless crops. Here and there parties of the little yard-high griffas toiled between the rows, with the rain dripping from their silver fur as they worked. Occasionally a man in a long waterproof coat and a shovel-shaped hat was to be seen striding from one group to another and inspecting progress. Another part of his uniform was a whip.

'Well, they've got some results to show,' he said, looking back at the smudge from the metal mills, almost hidden now by rain and mist.

'Yes, they've got that,' the man admitted. 'That's the griffas mostly – the donkey-work, I mean. There's plenty of griffas – all you like to round up in the forests. Lucky for you and me.'

'How?' asked Bert.

'On account of they need us to supervise. The griffas won't work without. So it's no good having unlimited griffas without men to look after them. That makes Chris Davey's buddies think twice before they wipe a man out. Take me. I'm what they call a subversive element – and I'd not be here now if they didn't need all of us they can get to look after the griffas. It was even worth bringing your lot from Mars.'

'And what do the griffas get out of it?' Bert asked.

'The chance to live a little longer – if they work,' said the man.

Bert made no comment on that. He sat looking out at the blanched landscape through the drizzling rain. Presently the train jerked itself aside on to a loop in the single line, and settled down to wait for a bit. His neighbour offered him a roll of the curious local bread. Bert thanked him, and bit into it. For a time they champed in silence, then the man said:

'Not what you expected, eh? Well, it's not what any of us expected. Still, it's all we've got.'

'Huh!' grunted Bert, non-committally.

His mind had been wandering very far away. He had been back in his old ramshackle boat idling along the canal. In his ears was the friendly chug of the engine mingled with the tinker-bell chimes. The thin, crisp air of Mars was in his lungs again. Beyond the bank red sands rolled on to low mountains in the distance. Somewhere ahead was a water-wheel that would surely be needing attention. Beside it a ruined tower of carved red stone. When he walked towards it the bannikuks would come bounding out of their holes, clinging and squeaking, and pestering him for nuts. In the doorway of the tower Zaylo

84

would be standing in a bright coloured dress, the silver pins shining in her hair, her eyes serious, her lips slightly smiling . . .

'No,' he added. 'Not what I expected.' He paused, then he added. 'How did it get this way?'

'Well, the Administrator here was okay with authority behind him – but without it he was nothing. Chris Davey saw that right off, and moved fast. The only serious opposition came from Don Modland who wanted a democratic set-up. But Don disappeared quite soon, and that had a kind of discouraging effect all round. So Davey and his mob took over. They built the seraglio stockade for the safety of the women and children – they said. If you're one of Davey's mob, that's where you live. If you're not, you never see the inside of the place. You only think you may – one day.

'Maybe it is true what they say about the birth rate and the death rate in there. Likely it's not. There's no way of checking. The place is guarded. It'd be hard to get in – harder still to get out, alive. If you're one of Davey's mob you carry a gun – if you're not, you don't. The long and the short of it is that if the results are coming along Chris doesn't trouble how his buddies get them.'

'He's made himself kind of – king of Venus?' Bert suggested.

'That's about it. This part of Venus, anyway. He's sitting pretty, with everything the way he wants it. The doggone thing is that whether you like it or not, he's making a job of it. He *is* building the place up – in his way.

'One of the things his buddies put out is that it's a race between us and the Slav lot down in the south. If they get ahead, and come beating through the tropics some way, it's going to be bad for us. So it's better for us to get ahead.'

'And attack them, you mean?'

'That's the way of it – sometime, when we're ready.'

A train came clattering past on the other loop. Small open trucks loaded with produce, others full of iron-ore, some travelling pens packed with silvery griffas, a couple of glass-windowed carriages on the end. Their own train started off again with a series of jolts. Bert continued to look out of the window. His companion's hand came down on his knee.

'Cheer up, son. We're still alive, anyway. That's more than you can say for most.'

'I was alive on Mars,' said Bert.

'Then why did you come here?' asked the other.

Bert tried to explain it. He did his best to convey his vision of an Earth reborn. The other listened sympathetically, with a slightly wistful expression.

'I know. Like the Old Man said: " – a new nation conceived in liberty and dedicated to the proposition that all men are created equal – ".'

'Something like that,' Bert agreed.

'Son,' said the other man, 'you were very young when you left Earth.'

'I was twenty-one,' said Bert.

'Twenty-one's still trailing clouds of glory – for all it thinks it knows. It was a grand thing the Old Man said, but have you ever thought how many empires had to grow up and be knocked out, or how many billions of poor guys had to die in slavery before a man could get up and say that?'

'I hadn't,' Bert admitted. 'But it *has* been said. So why can't this be a "nation conceived in liberty"?'

'Well, I guess perhaps the Old Man didn't have quite the right phrase, maybe. You see, after a creature is conceived, it has to go through all the stages – kind of recapitulate its evolution before it can get born.'

'That doesn't sound much like a subversive element talking,' said Bert.

'You don't have to be in a hurry to be subversive. All you got to do is to say "why?" when it ought to be "yes". If you keep on saying it you find yourself booked for another spell of managing griffas in the quarries, the way I am now.'

'But there's no reason to go back to the primitive. What's been said and worked out is all there in the books – books that are here on Venus. What I've seen for myself and what you've told me goes against it all. The thing they've set up is something like an ancient slave-state. We all know there's a better way of life than that – so, for God's sake, what's happening? With all the knowledge from Earth behind them, and the chance to build a new Earth here, surely they aren't going to pour half history down the drain?'

The other man looked at him for some moments before he answered, then he said:

'Son, I guess you've got it kind of wrong. Building a new Earth is just what they are doing. What you're complaining about is that they've not started building a new heaven.'

Bert regarded him more closely.

'I don't get that. I can remember Earth, you know.'

'Me too. The difference is, like I said, the clouds of glory. What did you do there?'

'I went to school, then to college, then to the School of Spacetraining.'

'And me. I worked on buildings, in factories, in ships, on docks, in spaceports, on railroads. I bummed around quite a stretch. Do you reckon I got to know what Earth was like my way – or was your way better?'

Bert sat silent a while, then he said:

'There were fine cities, happy people, music – and fine men, too.'

'Ever seen an iceberg? The part you *do* see looks mighty pretty in the sunshine.'

'There was enough to show the way a world might be, and ought to be.'

'Sure, sure. We all know the way things ought to be. We all got our little heavens.' He paused contemplatively. Looking at Bert again, he added: 'Maybe – one day. We *have* come quite a way in a few thousand years – but we've still got to grow up. Takes time, son, takes time.'

'But here things are *wrong*. They're going back. They seem to have forgotten all the things we've learned. We have to go *on*, not back. Now the people on Mars –'

'Sure. Tell me about Mars, son. That's one place I never was.'

Bert went on telling him about Mars. About the place itself, about the way the people, for all the simple poverty of their lives, seemed to enjoy life as a gift in itself, not as a means to something else, and were happy that way.

The little train rattled along. A dim line of hills ahead became visible through the drizzle, but Bert did not see them. His sight was all nostalgic. It showed red deserts set with placid canals, green patches about little homesteads. Somehow he found himself telling the stranger about Zaylo . . .

The stranger said nothing. Once or twice he made as if to ask a question, but let it go unspoken. Bert talked on, oblivious of the compassion in the listener's eyes.

They were almost at the end of the line before the other broke in on Bert's mood. He pointed out of the window at the hills now quite close. In places the green-grey vegetation on the slopes was scarred with the dark marks of workings.

'There's where we'll be doing our jobs,' he said.

Presently the train jerked to a stop. Bert stood up, heavily and wearily. He collected his gear, and followed the other man into the drizzling rain. He felt bowed down by his load. His feet shuffled in a clumsy trudge. He wondered how long it was going to take his muscles to adapt to Venus. At present the place bore down as heavily upon his flesh as upon his spirit . . .

Bert stood on the lip of a small quarry, surveying the scene beneath him. Because, rather remarkably, it was not raining he had an extensive view. But because it was likely to resume raining at any moment he still wore the long waterproof coat that was practically a local uniform. Beneath it his feet showed in large boots that were clumsy, but did keep out the wet. At his waist was a belt supporting a machete and a sheath-knife on the left. His other instrument, a whip, with its twelve-foot lash carefully coiled, was thrust into the belt on his right hand side.

Looking down almost between his feet he could see his party of fifty griffas at work. They were loading ironstone into small trucks which they would presently push on to the slope which led down to the terminus of the line, and later wind up again. Beyond the sheds and tangle of trucklines at the terminus itself he could see the electrified line, flanked all the way by cleared and cultivated fields, stretching like a rather uncertain swathe cut to the horizon. To either side the natural Venusian forest grew untouched. Mostly it was a monotone of the pallid and, to unaccustomed eyes, unhealthy looking grey-green. There was a little relief here and there from the pink flush of the displeasing plant they called the mock-rose – it reminded Bert more of a spiky petalled dahlia which had been swollen to some eight feet in diameter. Even more scattered, but giving some relief were occasional streaks of true green, and blobs of slatey-blue. Pennant-trees reared their crests magnificently above the ruck with their ribbons streaming. Still higher rose the feather-tops, swinging in great graceful arcs even in so light a wind. With the rippling fronds of the tree-ferns they helped to give the illusion that the whole plain was in undulating motion. Bert, pensively regarding the span from the mist-hidden sea in the east to the shadowy mountains in the west, loathed each acre of it individually and intensely.

The only things in sight he didn't loathe were griffas. For them he had a mixture of pity and fellow-feeling. They were intelligent little creatures, but the general opinion was that they were dead lazy. As Bert saw it, that just showed narrow thinking. Laziness is a relative term to be measured against work. Nobody calls a flower or a tree lazy. The point was that a wild griffa never had any conception of work. When it was caught and shown work, it didn't like it. Why should it? The captives netted by a drive in the forest came in as sad-eyed, bewildered little figures, of whom a number went promptly into a decline and allowed themselves to die. The rest had no great will to survive. Life in captivity was very little better to them than no life at all. The only thing that made them work at all was the desire to avoid pain. They were intelligent enough to be taught quite complicated duties, but what no one had been able to instil into them was the sacred idea of duty itself. They could not be brought to the idea that it was something they owed to these human invaders of their planet. It was Bert's job to keep them working by the only effective method. He loathed that, too.

There was also the uneasy feeling that his position in Venusian society was not all that different from theirs ...

His wandering thoughts were brought back by the sight of the foreman overseer climbing the path to the quarry. Bert descended to meet him.

The man gave him no greeting. He was dressed like Bert himself save for the sign of authority represented by the pistol on his belt. As he strode into the working it was plain that he was in a bad temper. His hard eyes looked Bert over with the full insolence of petty authority.

'Your lot's down on production. Way down. Why?' he demanded. But he did not seem to expect an answer. He glanced round, taking the place in at a sweep. 'Look at 'em, by God! Your job here is to keep the little rats working, isn't it? Well, why in hell don't you do it?'

'They're working,' said Bert, flatly.

'Working, hell!' said the overseer.

He drew his whip. The lash whistled. A female griffa screamed horribly, and dropped where she stood. Her two companions, linked by chains to her ankles, stood quivering, with fear and misery in their dark eyes. The rest, after a startled pause, began to work very much more actively. Bert's hand clenched. He looked down on the fallen griffa, watching the red blood well up and soak into the silver fur. He raised his eyes to find the overseer studying him.

'You don't like that,' the man told him, showing his teeth.

'No,' said Bert.

'You've gone soft. Building this place up is a man's job. When you've been here a bit you'll learn.'

'I doubt it,' said Bert.

'You'd better,' the overseer said, unpleasantly.

'I didn't come here to help build a slave-state,' Bert told him.

'No? You'd just like to start at the top – with none of the dirty work – wouldn't you? Well, it can't be done. You tell me one great nation or empire on Earth that didn't have this behind it at one stage?' He swung his whip with a crack like a rifle shot. 'Well, tell me – ?'

'It's *wrong*,' said Bert, helplessly.

'You know a better way? Love and kindness, maybe?' the man said, jeering. 'You've gone soft,' he repeated.

'Maybe,' Bert admitted. 'But I still say that if there's no better way of building than driving these creatures crazy with pain and fear until they die – then it's not worth doing at all.'

'Tchah! Where's your bible, Preacher? There's just one way to get the work that's got to be done, and this is it.'

His whip whistled again. Another little griffa screamed, and another.

Bert hesitated a second. Then he drew his own whip. The lash sang through the air and wrapped itself around the overseer's neck. At that moment Bert yanked on the handle with all his strength. The man lurched towards him, tripped on a chunk of ironstone, and came down on his head. Bert dropped the whip, and dived to stop him drawing his pistol.

His leap was superfluous. The overseer was not in a condition where he would be able to use a pistol – or a whip – any more.

The griffas had stopped work, and stood staring as Bert got up and fixed the holstered pistol to his own belt. He raised his eyes from the man on the ground and stared back at them. He turned and went towards the toolshed. There he took down the long-handled pincers that were customarily used to cut a dead griffa free from his fellows. Then he went back to them, and got to work.

When it was over they still stood round puzzled, with dark, sorrowful eyes blinking at him from silver-furred faces.

'Go on, you mugs! Beat it! Shoo!' said Bert.

He watched them scuttle away and disappear into the dense growth above the quarry, and then turned to reconsider the fallen man. The overseer was heavily built. It was laborious to Bert's still unaccustomed muscles to drag him out of the quarry, but he managed it. A short way down the path he paused a little to recover his breath. Then, with a great effort, he lifted the body, and heaved it into a mock-rose. The petal-like tendrils received the weight with a slow, engulfing movement like the yielding of a feather-bed. The large outer leaves began to close. Presently the thing was a hard tight ball looking like an enormous, etiolated Brussels sprout.

Bert sat down on a stone for ten minutes, regaining his strength, and thinking carefully. Then he stood up, with decision. But before he left he went back into the quarry to fetch his hat, for it had started to rain again.

Once the acceleration was over, Bert emerged from his hiding place and mingled with the rest. A full hour passed before someone tapped him on the shoulder and enquired:

'Say, what the hell are you doing here?'

The Captain and the Chief Officer regarded him uncertainly as he was brought before them. The pistol he wore was almost a badge of rank in itself.

'What's the trouble?' Bert enquired, blandly.

'You're not listed. How did you get here?' the Chief Officer enquired.

Bert looked surprised.

'Not listed? Somebody must have slipped up. They only put me on this job yesterday. But they said you'd been informed already, Captain.'

'Well, I hadn't. And what is "this job"?'

'It's – er – well, kind of recruiting-sergeant. You see I can speak four Martian dialects, and get along in several more.'

'Recruiting Martians, you mean?'

'That's the idea. Spin 'em the yarn, and bring 'em along. They'll be useful managing griffas if nothing else.'

He looked steadily back at the Captain as he spoke, hoping

that it would not occur to him that a Martian transferred to Venus would only be able to crawl about, if he weren't actually pinned flat by the gravitation. It did not. Probably the man had never even seen a Martian. He merely frowned.

'I should have been informed,' he said stiffly.

'Bad staff work somewhere,' Bert agreed. 'But you could get radio confirmation,' he suggested.

'Do you *know* anything of radio conditions on Venus?' enquired the Chief Officer shortly.

'No, but on Mars we –'

'Maybe, but Mars isn't Venus. Well, since you are here, you'd better make yourself useful on the trip.'

'Aye, aye, sir,' agreed Bert, briskly.

By the look of it no one had touched the old boat since he had moored her. Bert patted the engine, and then primed it. A pull-up or two, and she started. He laughed aloud. The old phut-phut-phut was like music to set his feet dancing. He cast off. In the old seat, with his arm over the tiller, he chugged out on the great canal.

Beyond the junction, and on a smaller canal, he stopped. From a locker in the cabin he produced old, patched clothes and a pair of the crude shoes that he was accustomed to make for himself. Overboard went the clothes they had given him on Venus, and the heavy, laced boots with them. He hesitated over the pistol, and then threw it after them – nobody used or needed such a thing on Mars. He felt lighter as he watched them sink. The miseries of the last few weeks on Venus, the long journey back from the quarries to the Settlement when he dared to move his weary body only by night for fear of being seen, the long wait in hiding close to the landing ground, the keeping alive on shoots and roots, the perpetual wet misery of the rain which scarcely ever let up, the anxious waiting for the return of the *Rutherford* A4, the delay while she was being made ready for her third and last trip of the conjunction, and, finally, the nervous business of smuggling himself aboard – all these began to become a bad dream.

He hitched his trousers, and tied them with a piece of cord. He was bending over the engine to restart it when the sound of a sudden thunder came rolling across the desert.

Bert looked back.

Above the horizon a plume of black smoke rose and expanded. He nodded in a satisfied way. The *Rutherford* A4 would not be taking part in any more slaving expeditions.

He whistled gently to himself as he coaxed the engine into action again.

It was the mind's eye picture come to life – even to the squeak pitched above the tinkerbell chimes telling that the waterwheel needed attention. As he walked towards the broken tower there was the familiar thump-thump of Annika, Zaylo's mother, at her work of pounding grain. The bannikuks scampered up, pestering – only this time he had no nuts for them, and they wouldn't seem to understand that. Annika rested her stone pestle as he approached.

'Hullo, Earthman,' she said. Her eyes searched his face keenly. 'You have been ill?' she added.

Bert shook his head, and sat down on a stone bench.

'I've been thinking,' he said. 'Remember last time I was here you said that if Earth was re-created now it would be stranger to me than Mars?'

'So it would, Earthman.'

'But I didn't believe you.'

'Well – '

'I think I see what you meant now.' He paused. 'Back home,' he went on, 'we used to talk about men and women we called saints – the funny thing about them was that they never seemed very real. You see, once they were dead, people agreed only to remember the good things about them. Seems to me – well, it might be there never was a place like the Earth I remembered . . . '

Annika nodded.

'A heaven behind you is no good,' she said. 'A heaven ahead is better. But to make a heaven around you is best.'

'You understand things, Annika. I was like a rich man who had been cheated out of all his money – the only worthwhile thing seemed to be to get it all back.'

'And now – ?' asked Annika.

'Now, I've stopped fooling myself. I don't want it. I've stopped crying for the moon – or the Earth. I'll be content to live and enjoy living. So this time – ' He broke off.

Zaylo, coming out of the door in the tower base, had paused there at the sight of him. She stood quite still for a moment, poised with the grace of a young goddess. The coils of her dark hair shone like lacquer, her misted copper skin glowed in the sunlight. She put her hand to her breast, her eyes sparkled with sudden pleasure, her lips parted . . .

Zaylo was not quite as he had pictured her. She was ten times more wonderful than anything memory could contrive.

'So this time,' Bert repeated. 'This time I have come to stay.'

The Venus Adventure

You may have read in the history books of Joseph Watson or, as he later called himself, Noah Watson; but it is probably that you have not found more than a slanting reference to his exploit. History is like that. As we go on with a longer and longer written record behind us, either events must be fore-shortened and incidents dropped out, or else the earlier centuries must be lopped from our knowledge.

It is too much for any but a specialist or a group of specialists to study all the strange phenomena of human history. We have, therefore, in this year, 2926 AD, chosen the former expedient of compressing our knowledge and whittling it down to the main facts and causes, with the inevitable result that many figures, once of world importance, are now remembered only in the museum libraries.

No one, save perhaps his own followers, could have ascribed world importance to Joseph Watson, but there can be no doubt that he was a remarkable figure in his day.

He was born in Scotland in May, 2104. It was a natural birth, for in the more rural northern districts the people still clung with a Puritan obstinacy to the superstitious belief that an incubated child was bound to be abnormal in some way. The Anti-Incubation Society's pamphlets with their spurious and harmful 'proofs' that no incubated child could possibly be considered to have a soul, were distributed in enormous numbers and with telling effect among the partly educated and the simple-minded. Such a prejudice dies hard and, even today, one sometimes hears of atavism to the extent of natural birth occurring in the obscurer corners of the earth.

Watson's mother paid the penalty for her crudity and credulity by dying at the birth of her son – a very frequent sequel to such a primitive mode of reproduction, as will be well understood – and the fact that she handed her life on to

95

him seems to have had a profound effect on his character. He is reported all through his schooldays to have been an 'erratic youth, given to introspection and not without flashes of misleading genius.' The phrase 'misleading genius' is puzzling, but there is little doubt that it refers to his strange, retrogressive mental outlook frequently shown by a firm adherence to principles long exploded.

It was during his university career that he entered upon a form of enthusiasm which will be understandable to few persons today, and therefore requires some explanation.

In 2123, the belief which all the world holds today, that of the Fundamental Order or Prime Origins, was known only to a small group. The rest of humanity grasped only a fragment of this whole and each section of people interwove its particular fragment with a different set of customs and superstitions to produce what it called a 'religion'. These 'religions', it must be understood, had all of them the same basis but differed in form according to the climate and the ancestry of the different races. Thus there would be found in the colder countries a hardy and stern 'religion', and in the warmer zones, a more colourful, less practical belief.

Joseph Watson, a Puritan at heart, gathered around himself a similarly-minded group and left his university with the firm determination to start a 'Revival'.

He began his campaign with the powerful backing of the Anti-Incubation Society. Quite what mental twist led him to ally himself with the very body whose pamphlets were responsible for his mother's death, it is difficult to understand, but there can be no doubt that its views gave him his later warcry of 'What's natural's right'.

From the very beginning his meetings were a success. An eye-witness of one of the earliest wrote: 'The great, gaunt figure of Joseph Watson as he appeared on the platform would have impressed any man. He started to speak with a deceptive quietness of voice and mildness of manner, but as he continued this wore away.

'His mane of fair hair tossed and shook with the emphasis of his gestures and his deep, Scottish voice boomed sonorously through the hall. His eyes took on a fire as his enthusiasm rose and it was hard to believe that they did not look out beyond the audience at some mystic vision. I can safely assert that there was not a man nor a woman in all the great gathering who was not at least temporarily held under his sway.'

Watson climbed from triumph to triumph. His meetings became occasions for turning out special police to control the crowds. Even the overflow halls were besieged by throngs who struggled to hear him, if only through a loudspeaker. The Anti-Incubation Society began to develop an active following in Scotland numerically surpassing its wildest dream. Money poured into its war chests until it became a power to be reckoned with. Nor was it alone in reaping the golden harvest which Watson's voice fostered.

'What's natural's right,' Watson would roar and then proceed to trounce the vivisectionists, the vaccinationists, the birth-controllers, the alcohol drinkers, the smokers, the gamblers, before winding up the exhibition with another blow at his old enemies, the incubationists.

At the end of each meeting he would drop his ferocity with a suddenness which took his audience by surprise, and kneel in prayer.

In three years his own supporters were raised to such peaks of enthusiasm that they made Scotland too hot to hold him.

A mob in Glasgow went straight from one of his meetings to the local Incubation Home and wrecked the place from cellar to roof. Not only was the damage to property consider-able, but the outrage started a controversy which was debated hotly all over the civilised world. Briefly, the problem raised was: 'Is it, or is it not, murder, to destroy a foetus which is developing in its incubating tank?'

A similar attack was made on the Edinburgh Home. The crowd was beaten off with casualties, but a number of police were killed outright.

In Dundee, Watson's too enthusiastic followers attempted to enforce prohibition by the simple expedient of wrecking all licensed premises. Whole streets were wet with spilled drink and a policeman's head seemed as good a place to smash a bottle as any other.

The Government decided to take action and warrants were issued for the arrest of Joseph Watson as the instigator of unrest in most of the towns and cities of Scotland. But the warrants were never executed for Watson chose to disappear. The Government was saved a great deal of trouble by his action.

He is next heard of in America, some seven years later. The date of his arrival and the manner in which he filled the intervening time must remain forever a mystery. Furthermore, he was no longer Joseph Watson, but had become Noah Watson, though whether by his own design, or by gradually acclimating to a nickname, is doubtful. It remains, however, quite certain that Joseph and Noah were one and the same: no one who had once seen him could mistake the man.

He was still reforming and still trouncing those sections of the community who attempted to improve on nature, but now he was even more general in his accusations of wickedness and more fiery in his breathings of warnings about the 'wrath to come'. Somewhere during the last few years he had picked up a seed of thought which grew in his fertile mind to the conviction that the world was due to end very soon, or if not to end, at least to be punished for its wickedness in some catastrophic and highly unpleasant manner.

It seems odd to us now that a man should be able to believe such a thing – not only believe it himself, but persuade others of its truth. Nevertheless, it must be remembered that in the twenty-second century knowledge of our world was, like many other forms of knowledge, in an extremely rudimentary state. It was even easy for anyone to predict the end of the world and find educated persons to accept the prophecy without the slenderest data.

Watson would never reveal whence he obtained his information of the imminence of a 'judgment day' by earthquake. He said merely that it was coming and soon. He called upon everyone to repent, claiming that each was a sinner though he might not know it.

'Noah,' said this new Noah, 'was sent to warn the world before the Flood. You have read what happened to those who did not heed him. Now I have a warning for you. Do you forget the way in which they mocked Noah? Do you mean to mock my warning too?'

But his second campaign did not repeat the success of his Scottish days. Perhaps it lacked the sentimental appeal. Perhaps his moment was not well-chosen. His meetings, though vast, lacked the worshipping silence of those former gatherings where the audience hung upon each word. Now, some even came to scoff; it was one of these who cut in on him with the question: 'Where's your Ark, Noah?'

A number of persons laughed. Watson faltered in his speech and lost the thread of his whole discourse as he was greeted with cries from all parts of the building: 'Yes, where's your Ark? Show us your Ark, Noah.' Someone at the back started to sing 'The Animals went in Two by Two', and for a while, the meeting was in an uproar.

Watson, for one of the few times on record, lost his temper.

'I've got an Ark,' he roared. 'I've got an Ark and when it saves me you'll be sorry you didn't believe. You won't be inside it – you'll be burning, all of you.'

Watson was telling the truth. He had an Ark.

In 2133, at the beginning of his 'end of the world' campaign, he had contrived somehow to meet Henry Headington and right from the start he had managed to impress that gentleman. Headington was among the richest men in the world. His aircraft factory in Chicago had netted him such a fortune that his wealth could never be accurately estimated. Or rather it should be said that by the time the computation was complete, the value of the holdings had altered to a degree which rendered the estimate useless. He was hedged around, as were all wealthy men of his time, with secretaries and guards, but Watson had not only approached him but enlisted him as a supporter.

II

INTO THE UNKNOWN

Henry Headington was not a great deal interested about the future of his soul, about which Watson appeared to worry so much, but he was concerned at the possible results to his comfortable existence should the earth indeed blow up. In the course of the many serious consultations which took place between the two, Headington became more and more convinced until his belief in the imminent catastrophe grew firm as Watson's own. But Henry was a man of different mettle. At the end of one sitting, he slowly removed his cigar (of which Watson disapproved) and regarded the other impressively.

'You talk a lot,' he said. 'You get around telling people to repent. Maybe they will, maybe they won't, either way it's not going to help them a lot when it comes to a flare-up. Of course, talking's your line and I don't blame a man for following his line, but it's not mine. I don't talk things; I do 'em.'

That was Headington's way. His experts were all assembled and instructed, and within a few weeks the first fruits of their labour began to appear in the shape of a gigantic shed raising itself in a corner of the Headington Experimental Rocket-Drome. Throughout the Headington concerns there was more than a little speculation as to its purpose. Obviously the hangar was intended for a craft of a size hitherto unattempted. Rumours crept out and flew around, as rumours always will.

It was reported as an intention to build the biggest strato-sphere plane in the world. Others gave it as their opinion that old man Headington had gone mad and wanted to get to the moon. The opinion of all outside the knowledgeable few was that the machine would be a colossal failure. Probably such a huge bulk would never lift from the earth, and even if it did the pay-load would be infinitesimal.

But the work went steadily ahead. The designers sweated in their offices, bending over intricate plans and drawing till their backs and eyes ached. They may have been sceptical of their power to fulfil the boss's demands to the letter, but they did not show it. The pay was good, but even more important to men who had spent all their lives complying with government aircraft regulations, was the allowance of a free hand. No longer were they bound by the Governmental restrictions regarding noise, power to bulk ratio, size and position of crew's quarters, multiplicity of safety devices where one efficient instrument would serve, and all the other hundred and one trials of their profession.

The object this time was perfection and no worry about working to cost limits. All Headington's fortune was behind them if they wanted it. And so they feverishly drew with the delirious intoxication of the power to make their dreams come true.

The pattern-makers at the foundries were presented with problems which caused them to swear and scratch their heads, but then they too caught the enthusiasm of the designers and solved each difficulty as it came. The instrument builders were asked to produce such gauges and measures that their heads ached with inventive effort. The metallurgists gleefully produced the formulae of alloys previously considered too expensive to be of any practical use, and gradually a huge bulk began to grow inside its huger shed.

Headington had developed a simple faith in Watson which raised the latter to a combination position of a minor prophet and a good-luck mascot. He was insistent that the reformer should attend the keel-laying ceremony of the great ship and make frequent visits to observe the progress of the work.

'She's going to be a marvel. Nothing like her has been tried in the history of the world,' the millionaire said proudly.

'The *Ark*,' murmured Watson. There was a far-away look in his eyes as though he stared back through history at that other Ark waiting to save the faithful.

The *Ark*, when finished, was condemned by every government inspector, without exception. It was not even permitted a trial flight and some went as far as to recommend its destruction lest someone were tempted to create a public danger by taking it up. Headington's money and influence served to dispel the danger of the latter threat being carried into execution, but even his backing failed to accomplish the granting of a licence for the craft.

So the *Ark* stood untested in its shed for many months. It was kept fully-provisioned and loaded to its limit with fuel and supplies of all kinds. The owner's faith in Watson never wavered, even many of the mechanics and engineers were converted from their former scoffing, but the *Ark* itself gradually became a laughing-stock for the world. Photographs of its stupendous shed occurred in newspapers everywhere. Misinformed articles on its builder's hopes, fears and intentions were sure of a ready sale. Watson encountered increasing jeers at his meetings once his association with Headington was known, and the two of them figured frequently in popular cartoons. The world, in fact, treated the new *Ark* much in the same way as it had treated the old.

Then Watson's wife, a woman as inflammatory as her husband, publicly announced that she had been granted a vision.

'And in my vision,' she cried, 'I saw the world spew forth flames. It was split asunder on account of its wickedness and from the great clefts its fiery life surged out, turning the oceans to clouds of steam, rolling over the land in a wave of fire which melted the very mountains in its path. And as I stood in awe of the great punishment visited upon evil-doers, a voice seemed to whisper in my ear. "November," it said, "November the twenty-second." '

It is impossible in these well-ordered days for us to appreciate the weight carried by such an unsupported assertion. Some were wise enough to take no notice of the woman's raving, but the names of Headington and Watson were so much in the public ear that the report was circulated all over the world to become in many a distant land the subject of apprehensive speculation or the cause of sceptical laughter.

But there was one group which took it seriously, neither arguing nor debating, but accepting it as a fact. Headington forced on what final preparations were necessary with a growing agitation since it was already late September. Watson grew more impassioned and his meetings became wilder until it was rare for them to end without the intervention of the police. There is a description of him in those last days throwing out his arms in gestures of the most violent oratory while his wife knelt before him on the platform, facing the audience and praying it to repentance.

A month before the catastrophe was due, the police forbade the holding of any more meetings, and Watson and his wife passed from the public sight.

The night of the twenty-first of November, 2134, was long remembered. All over the world groups of nervous persons remained watching and praying with an irrational sense that death was better met fully clad than in night clothes, even if it be instantaneous destruction.

An observer of the final scenes in the great shed of the *Ark* luckily remained alive to tell of the events he saw there.

'Headington had gathered together all his family, most of his engineers and designers and their families and even many of the workmen in addition to the crew and its relatives. All were aboard and ready save for a small knot of watchers to one side of the colossal flier.

'Once midnight had struck, the whole shed was heavy with an apprehensive silence. The group comprising Headington, Watson, Mrs. Watson and one or two more hung breathlessly over a solid stone table. Their eyes never for a moment left the needle of a seismograph for which it served for a mounting base.

'At the end of an hour the silence was so ominous that one

would have given a mint of money for the relief of breaking it, but still nobody spoke. Occasionally the sound of someone moving uneasily inside the vessel's entrance port rustled out into the shed to disturb the tomb-like stillness.

'There was a sudden intake of breath. Had the needle kicked? The group bent still closer. The needle kicked once more, definitely and decisively. The end had come. There was a wild stampede into the shining safety of the *Ark*.'

There is little need to tell most people how the *Ark* left. How the passengers were in such terror that they even neglected to open the doors of the shed. How the shed itself was so shattered by the impact that it collapsed killing most of those left within. But there can seldom have been a more gorgeous and awe-inspiring sight than that monstrous rocket as it took off. A curving tail of fire spread golden behind it lighting the country-side with the glare of a man-made comet. Scorching the earth beneath it, it passed in glory: head-on for the stars.

The rocket did far more harm as it went than had been caused by the small subsea earthquake in the Pacific a few minutes before. Many imaginations played with its probable fate, but no evidence came to support them, and gradually, like a million other incidents of history, it slipped into the all but forgotten past.

Some maintained that it had managed to leave the sphere of Earth's attraction and that such a feat, once accomplished, could be performed again, but no one knew how. The chemists, the designers, the engineers had gone with their ship and their knowledge had gone with them.

It was not until Hal Newton made his famous expedition that any knew for certain the fate of the *Ark*.

III

THE FIRST PLANS

The story of Hal Newton's exploit properly begins more than a year after he married Davida Jonson or, as she is now known the world over, Vida. The two had left their incubators within a month of one another. They had played together as children and grown up with their brilliant minds racing until in the spring of the year 2920 they had decided to pull together.

Hal passed out of his college the youngest rocket-pilot ever created. The thunder of the rockets was the throb of life to him and he handled his planes as though there existed an understanding between himself and the machinery.

Vida was little less outstanding in her chosen calling of chemist. She slid through her classes collecting the envy and amazement of her professors, for she seemed to learn in months what others painfully acquired in years. Already, at twenty-four, she had interesting discoveries behind her and a future of brilliant promise. It was given to her to leap where others plodded.

The marriage was scarcely popular in their set; there were too many broken hearts at Vida's feet and too many sighs behind Hal's back, but none could doubt that the match would be a success.

For a year the two pursued their occupations as before. Hal hurtling through the sky, his body still no higher than the stratosphere while his imagination, as ever, reached out to the stars. Vida coercing her chemicals and dreaming of a future far different from that which fate held in store.

Then the great Gordon Jonson, Vida's father, died, and all his millions came to her.

On July the fifth, 2922, the great Newton venture received the first gentle push which was to launch it into space.

The Newtons and their guests finished an excellent dinner and adjourned for coffee and cigarettes to their comfortable lounge. Hal had shown himself somewhat preoccupied during the meal and now he plunged into talk in the manner of one determined to get the matter off his chest.

'Vida and I have a proposition to lay before you people,' he said. 'It's not going to be a simple little jaunt so I don't ask any of you to give me your final answers at once – it is the kind of thing which will be better for thinking over.'

He surveyed his guests for a moment. There was Temberly, the biologist, barely thirty, but already going a little bald on the crown, short-sighted and sharply bird-like in his movements. Next to him sat the bulky Bill Crawshaw. Bill's father had been the last of the famous explorers and his son would no doubt have followed in his footsteps had there been a corner of the world left unexplored.

104

As things stood, he was forced to the substitute of roaming the earth, looking for trouble, an occupation at which he was said to excel both in finding and settling. Lastly there was Lucy Kramer with the face of a Madonna hiding under its placidity a genius for chemistry nearly equal to that of her co-worker, Vida.

'The proposal is this,' Hal continued. 'Vida has discovered a truly remarkable explosive which has, we think, solved the problem of opposing the earth's gravity. Ever since I was a kid, it has been my ambition to get out into space. With Vida's discovery and a special ship which I have almost finished designing, I think it can now be done.

'Now, the suggestion is this: are you willing to come with us?'

There was a moment's pause during which no one spoke: Hal went on:

'Of course it is impossible to tell you what the odds are against our ever returning. There are plenty of known dangers as well as the unknown, but Vida and I have enough faith in ourselves to risk them and we want to know if you have.'

The biologist looked at his host with an expression of doubt.

'Er – I don't quite see what I could usefully do in space. After all, I don't think it is likely that you will find any forms of life there – though, of course, you might,' he amended hastily.

Vida looked at him and smiled encouragingly.

'We don't expect to, but you see we don't intend to stay in space for long. We shall land.'

'Where?' demanded Temberly and Crawshaw simultaneously.

'On Venus,' Vida said as she cast a glance in her husband's direction.

'I had thought of Mars,' Hal admitted, 'but Vida's converted me. I think she's right when she says that it would be unwise on a first trip to land on a dead or dying world where there may be insufficient air. It is quite possible that some readjustments may have to be made before the return journey and that would prove awkward.'

'There's a chance of good sport there?' enquired Crawshaw.

'My dear Bill, how can I possibly tell you? At a rough guess I should say that you will probably be granted more than you expect. Venus is considered to be in a very primitive condition – it may be in a reptilian age. Trying to hit a brain the size of a walnut in an animal as big as a house ought to be a good test of marksmanship even with a rocket-shell rifle.'

Bill beamed.

'I'm your man, Hal.'

'Good. But don't hesitate if you want to reconsider it.'

'That's all right -- I shan't want to.'

'What do you think about it, Tem?' Hal asked.

Temberly's eyes wandered uncertainly round the room; he appeared to be seeking inspiration.

'Well – er – ' he began.

Vida broke in. After favouring her husband with a glance of irritation, she turned to the girl beside her.

'Lucy?'

'Of course.' Lucy spoke in a soft, deep voice which matched the calmness of her face.

Temberly was understood to mumble that he, too, would join the party.

The rest of the evening was spent in arranging responsibilities. Hal, of course, was to be chief pilot and he had his eye on a likely man called Heerdahl for a relief. The air conditioning plant, atmosphere testers, concentrated foods, etc., fell naturally into the province of Vida's and Lucy's interests. Crawshaw was to have charge of munitions and armaments and was with difficulty restrained from there and then delivering a lecture on the science of gunnery. Temberly went off into a brown study of contemplation as he made mental lists of his biological necessities.

'There must be someone whose job it is to keep a full account of the expedition,' Vida declared.

Crawshaw who had grown abstracted suddenly brightened.

'I know the very person for that job. Lots of experience and a good all-round general knowledge. Nobody better – if she'll come,' he ended doubtfully.

'She?' said Hal. 'What's all this, Bill? Who is she?'

'You must have heard of her – Freda Linden.'

Vida looked relieved. Bill Crawshaw had a reputation for being a little erratic in his friendships.

'I've met her,' she said. 'She'll probably come.'

'That leaves only three vacancies,' Hal observed. 'They must

106

be filled by technical men – say two engineers and an electrician.'

The party broke up late. Each had been allotted his or her part and accepted with a steadiness which warmed Hal's heart. As he watched the visitors drive off, he was full of an affection for these people who were going to help his dream towards realisation.

'You were right, darling. I ought to have known better than to ask Temberly before he knew what Lucy intended. When do you suppose those two idiots are going to do something about it?'

But Vida was not listening. There was a far-away look in her eyes.

'You know, dear, there is one thing we must do before we go off on this adventure.'

'Lots of things, darling. What's this particular one?'

'We must pay a visit to the home and see about renting an incubator.'

IV

ON VENUS

Setbacks and worries crowded thick and fast upon the Newtons during the next few months. Parts arrived below specification and had to be returned. The alloy for the exhaust tubes proved unequal to the strains it would have to bear. *Jonite*, Vida's new explosive had to be rendered more stable. But gradually, as the year wore on, the *Fyra* began to take shape.

Hal conducted the others over the ship and asked for their advice on points of interior fitments. In about one hundred feet of overall length they found several cabins; one main living-room with windows of fused quartz; a cooking galley and pantry and a small laboratory which would have to serve for the chemists, the biologist and the photographer as occasion demanded. Vida and Lucy criticised the cooking arrangements and demanded alterations, while Crawshaw stipulated for weapon racks to be fixed to certain walls 'just in case'.

Apart from such details, very little appeared to have escaped Hal's attention. They marvelled at the ingenious disposal of fuel tanks and the compactness of the machinery which was to undertake the stupendous task of shooting them through space. Crawshaw regarded the simple control-board and its attendant array of pressure dials for the different rocket exhausts, almost with misgiving. It looked, he thought, more like a typewriter and a collection of clocks than the nervous system control upon which they would all depend. But he shrugged his shoulders and moved on; engineering, electrical or otherwise was not in Crawshaw's line. He inspected the ammunition lockers and small-arm store with approval.

When they left the ship, it was to gaze up at the shining hull with a still greater respect for its marvels of compactness and comfort. The ship's name in large letters on the bow caught Crawshaw's eye.

'Why the *Fyra*?' he asked.

'It means "fiery" and this craft is going to have more fire in her than ever was gathered together before,' Hal explained.

At the end of June, 2923, she was declared ready for a trial flight – an unfortunate necessity. So far the work had progressed, if not in secret, at least without publicity, but the *Fyra*'s trials brought the Newtons on to the front page. Reporters saw the chance of a scoop in this new, winged ship which thundered through the skies at incredible speed. They saw it pass over as a gleam of silver with roaring red ports and, with hastily gathered information, they rushed to their desks.

'A new day has dawned in the history of aviation – '

'Epoch making discovery by young pilot – '

'Hitherto undreamed of speeds in the lower atmosphere have been attained by – ' they scribbled.

Hal refused to give any information to the newspapers. He was, he said, merely carrying out experiments and had no intention yet of publishing any results. Nevertheless, from an obscure source the truth leaked out. Hal Newton was to challenge space. Even the date of his intended departure was coaxed into print so that the world might gape at the adventurers.

'On August the twentieth Hal Newton will set out on his attempt to reach the moon,' said one paper with a magnificent disregard for accuracy.

People were no longer so sceptical as they had been, of man's ability to conquer space. They had become, in fact, so used to the idea that they were beginning to grow irritated over the many unsuccessful attempts which had been made. The papers gave lists of Hal's predecessors. There was Jornsen who had fallen into the Pacific. Craig who, like Headington, had never been heard of again. Drivers who had succeeded only to the extent of making his machine forever a satellite of Earth. Simpson who had fallen in Chicago and wrecked a fifth of the city in the resulting explosion: and the rest of the gallant army of would be explorers who had laid down their lives. Thanks to the efforts of the press, coupled with its own morbid desires to stare at doomed persons for the last time, an enormous mass of people surrounded Newton's flying ground on August the twentieth.

The crowd was more than annoyed when told that the *Fyra* had taken off the day before.

Hal had spread orders to his complement to be ready to start on the evening of the nineteenth, and to keep the date secret.

He and Vida were awaiting them aboard the ship. The first to come were the two excellent engineers, Mackay and Freeman. Then Heerdahl, the second pilot, arrived with a clatter in a single-seater sports rocket, a speedy and essentially unsafe machine of his own design. Bill Crawshaw loomed out of the night accompanying little Freda Linden who possessed half her escort's height and twice his assurance. Smith, the electrician, stumbled frantically on to the steps of the *Fyra* apologising breathlessly for his lateness, only to discover that he had mistaken the time. Lucy Kramer explained that Temberly had suddenly remembered some essential at the last moment, and dashed back for it. He turned up some ten minutes later in a depressed condition, having failed to find this important article.

'And that's the lot,' Hal said as he ran his eyes round the group. 'All ten of us. There's no point in delaying longer.'

He leaned out to wave farewell to the little bunch of pilots and engineers which stood enviously by, then withdrew and watched the door settle into its sealing gaskets.

'Couches everyone – and don't forget your safety straps.'

Vida pressed her husband's hand as he passed her on the way to his own slung couch. He gave her an encouraging smile.

'We'll make it, darling.'

He gave a final glance round the room to see that nothing swung loose.

'Ready?' he called.

All settled themselves as well as possible to resist the effects of acceleration. He fastened the safety strap around him and laid a hand on the control desk at his side.

'Here we go.'

He pressed a group of keys. Again a rocket of Earth's venturers shot out; head-on for the stars.

It is kinder to say little about the actual flight. No doubt means will one day be evolved to make such a journey more of a pleasure and less a test of endurance than it is at present. The human constitution is ill-adapted to withstand the effects of rapid acceleration or deceleration, and lack of gravity, while not so serious in its results produces extremely distressing reactions at first. Not until the *Fyra* was several days out could her occupants be certain that the eating of a meal would prove worth the trouble.

The effect of the start was little more than negligible on the two pilots and engineers. In their years of training and practice they had learned how best to resist and how to recover. Of the rest it may be said that there were torturing moments when they one and all wished that they had been left at home to die comfortably in bed. But, even with its failings, the human machine is the most adaptable form that we know. Not only that, but it has a special facility for unpleasantness of minimising it in retrospect.

Five days out, each was wondering why he had been so fussed about little discomforts and making mental vows that he never would be again. Vows to be as easily broken as made.

At first there was novelty to occupy the travellers. The great empty blackness of space with its myriad sparks of stars, the sun itself flaming and flaring undiffused, seeming away to one side as they travelled in a great curve to intersect with Venus's orbit. But the unchanging soon grows dull, and soon they left the fused windows to seek occupation.

Without exception they admit that the first fortnight aboard the *Fyra* was the cruellest test of nerves they had ever undergone. None felt well and all were insufficiently used to the surroundings to be able to settle down and forget the vast nothingness outside. Their restless minds were forever urging and willing the ship to greater speed in the anxiety to have done with the journey and to know what lay before them. Hal has written in his log of his admiration for the restraint they exercised to keep from breaking into open quarrels.

The worst period must drag to its end. Hal had calculated a month for the duration of the flight. When he was able to announce that the ship was up to time and that the fortnight had seen them past the halfway mark, it seemed as though that invisible milestone out in space had lifted a spell from the whole company. It was almost as if, until that moment, they had not believed in the reality of what they were doing nor in the fact that ahead, Venus indeed waited with tasks to be performed and problems to be solved. With one accord they woke from their dejection, threw off the lethargy and went to work.

Crawshaw overhauled his armoury. Temberly looked to his slides and specimen boxes. All began to accept weightlessness, with its attendant inconveniences, as a mere discomfort instead of a cause for permanent grumbling. Hal watched with satisfaction the morale of his ship improve. He had known that they were a good lot at heart for he had chosen them with care, but there were moments in the early part of the journey when he suffered from misgiving – perhaps he himself was not so unaffected by the monotony and cramped quarters as he thought.

Venus, at long last, hung like a great frosted globe close by. It had the appearance of a huge, fleecy ball for some of its surface was visible through the swathing of clouds. Eager eyes watched the planet incessantly for some revealing rift, but Venus was keeping her secrets till the last.

The *Fyra* had been gently decelerating for some days. After the strain caused by the start, Hal considered it wiser to treat his company to an easier stop. Not until they were comparatively close was it necessary to order:

'Couches everyone.'

With rockets blasting fiercely from her bow ports the *Fyra* began to nose down. Soon she was roaring through Venusian skies like a fiery dragon seeking a resting place on this alien planet.

The ship landed with only a slight concussion. She slithered for a few yards on her shining belly, lurched a trifle to one side and then settled to rest. The eagerness of the travellers caused them to forget the lingering discomforts of deceleration. There was a hasty unbuckling of safety straps followed by a rush across the sloping floor to the windows. A surprised silence was their first reaction to the strange world.

111

A soft white light filtered through the thick layer of clouds to reveal a queerly unfamiliar scene. They were resting almost in the centre of an oval space which appeared to be a natural clearing. It was dotted here and there only with low shrubs: further back the edge of a forest was visible. The trees were of moderate height and smooth-stemmed until they broke into a flourish of small, broad shoots at the top. The shoots appeared to be more fragile than branches, yet stronger than leaves.

Creepers were slung in great loops from each shock-headed tree to its neighbours and below grew a thickness of shrubbery, some ten to twelve feet high. Every one of the plants visible was different from anything they had known. Instead of the familiar soothing green of Earthly landscapes, they faced a vista where all was of the same white-grey colour. The trees, with their vague likeness to palms, the lesser bushes and even the bed of thick, twisted stalks which covered the whole clearing, all had that same look of being bleached and rendered lifeless by some all-pervading blight. The first inspection damped all spirits.

'Venusian grass is a pretty poor imitation of the real thing,' said Heerdahl peering at the foreground. 'Looks like a million fat, white worms frozen stiff.'

Vida shuddered slightly.

'It's not very welcoming,' she agreed. 'I can imagine all sorts of queer things creeping silently in that tangle of forest.'

Lucy's deep voice expressed the sensations which lurked in them all.

'It's a ghostly world, full of pale horrors. Nothing moves but a few curls of mist in the distance. You see, the leaves just hang tiredly, there's not a living breath to stir them. Perhaps any moment they will be parted by some grey ghost.'

Smith, the electrician, moved uneasily.

'Do you want to give us all the horrors?' he enquired. 'It looks bad enough without the spook stuff.'

Temberly who had been goggling wordlessly out of the window, suddenly turned and ran down the room.

'Hi. Where are you off to?' Hal called.

'Outside,' the little man replied, choking with excitement.

Hal dashed after him and caught him as his hand was on the opening lever of the main port.

'Steady on, man. You might kill us all. We've not tested the air yet. Vida,' he added, 'get your sample and tell us if it's safe.'

While they waited impatiently for the result of the analysis, Freda, with the help of Crawshaw, set up her large camera and started it clicking at the view.

'Might as well take a still and have done with it – it's a waste of movie film,' Crawshaw muttered disgustedly. He glowered out at the silent scene and added dejectedly to Hal: 'Where are all these monsters you talked about? I can't see anything more dangerous than a few washed-out cabbages.'

Hal smiled.

'I never knew a pair of people in such a hurry as you and Tem. He wants to dash out and pick plants without caring if he dies in the attempt, and your first thought on reaching a strange world is to start a massacre. You wait a bit, it looks as though there ought to be plenty for you to do in there.' He waved a hand to indicate the thicker, misty forest in the background.

'Oxygen content a little higher than normal, otherwise much the same as our own atmosphere,' came Vida's voice from the little laboratory. 'Quite safe, though rather dense. You'd better equalise the pressure in here slowly.'

Hal busied himself for a moment with gauges and then turned to address the rest.

'Now we've got to settle who is to go out on the first expedition and who stays with the ship. Temberly must come, of course, forcible restraint is the only alternative in his case. And we'll need Crawshaw with his weapons. Three people, at least, must stay on the *Fyra*. What about you, Smith?'

Smith nodded and cast a contemptuous glance at as much of Venus as was visible through the window.

'I'm quite willing to keep out of that stuff,' he said.

'I'll stay, too,' Lucy volunteered. 'It's more – more human in here.'

'That's two then. What about you, Freeman?'

Freeman glanced questioningly at Mackay.

'I guess we'll both stay if you don't mind,' said the latter.

'I might have known it,' Hal laughed. 'Has anyone ever succeeded in separating you two?'

'Not for long,' Mackay said with a grin.

'Right, then that's settled. You four stay and the rest of us make a short exploration tour. Bill, I think some machetes would be useful in that stuff.'

8

EXPLORING

It was a subdued party of six which tramped away towards the trees. The queer silence and lack of motion in their surroundings seemed to quell even the cheerful Heerdahl as they emerged from the *Fyra*.

Each was lightly-clad as a result of Hal's warning.

'The temperature isn't as high as we feared it might be. The air's so dense that it probably eases it off a bit. But we've got to remember that we're twenty-five million miles or so nearer the sun, so wear only essentials.'

Though shirts and shorts weighed little, they were encumbered with other necessarily heavy paraphernalia. All carried pistols in belt holsters and the men, save for Temberly, slung rocket-shell rifles across their backs. The little biologist was already so laden with two large, black specimen boxes that he could not be further impeded with the weight of a rifle. Hal carried several instruments including a short-range radio transmitter for communication with the *Fyra*. Freda was panniered on one side by film box and on the other by camera and firmly refused Crawshaw's offers to relieve her of their weight. Crawshaw, himself, and Heerdahl bore rucksacks containing a small quantity of food, while at their belts, as at Hal's, dangled heavy machetes.

The only sounds to break the stillness were those they made themselves; the rattle of accoutrements and the soggy, squashing noise as the fat tendrils covering the ground were crushed by their progress.

Temberly, after a rapid inspection of the growths underfoot, forged ahead with swinging specimen boxes in the direction of the forest.

'We'll have to keep an eye on him,' Vida said loudly.

Hal looked at her in surprise, wondering why she found it necessary to raise her voice.

'Yes. It'll be easy to get lost in that stuff,' he found himself shouting in reply.

Vida laughed at the startled expression with which he heard his own voice.

'It's this thick atmosphere. Makes things sound much louder,' she said.

'Well, this beats tombs for silence. I haven't heard a sound yet except the row we're making ourselves,' Heerdahl observed.

They reached the fringe of the forest, to catch up with Temberly who was staring in a puzzled manner at a curious plant.

'Look at this thing!' he cried excitedly.

'Ghastly looking object,' commented Crawshaw unimpressed. 'What's up with it? Looks the same beastly colour as all the rest, to me.'

'Well, it is a flower.'

'Humph. Try again,' Crawshaw advised.

'It is. It's just got two main petals – those upper and lower things looking like jaws.'

They all gazed at the growth. It measured some three feet across and its petals were indeed like jaws, giving an impression that an enormous head was gaping at them.

'You see,' said Temberly pointing eagerly inside, 'it has stamens with pollen on them.'

'Well, why not?' asked Crawshaw in bored tones.

'Even I can see that. It hasn't any colour to attract insects and cause pollination,' Freda said.

'But suppose the Venus insects hate colour – they might, you know?'

'Don't be a fool, Bill. Of course – '

'Incidentally, has anyone seen any insects?' Vida interrupted. Nobody had.

'It's very queer,' Temberly puzzled. 'I suppose there are no insects here, but in that case how does the thing manage to get fertilised?'

He peered more closely at the great, pallid flower and leaned over to gaze short-sightedly inside. He put one hand against the lower petal.

With a sudden swish the upper half swept down upon the lower, blowing a cloud of pollen into his face. The rest of the party laughed heartlessly at the sight of the little man choking and spluttering over the flower dust he had swallowed.

'Well, there's your answer, Tem,' said Vida. 'The plant is

very sensitive when it is touched. It blows out the pollen and hopes for the best.'

Temberly, recovered, regarded the plant with admiration, as though it had accomplished something very clever.

'Ingenious – most ingenious,' he said with the air of one paying a compliment. 'A sort of natural bellows.'

They paused while Freda took her photograph of the great flower, and then decided to work into the forest.

'We must keep close together. No dashing off to one side (particular application to Temberly). Remember, we don't yet know the period of Venus's rotation. There might be serious consequences if it were to grow dark suddenly and we were separated. You had better lead, Bill. You've got a machete in case of heavy going? Good. Now Temberly second, and for heaven's sake don't hold up the procession too much, you're going to have weeks to examine all this stuff. Everybody ready? Let's go.'

They forged ahead with but little conversation. Occasionally there was a pause while Crawshaw cleared a way through the soft growths and Freda seized another opportunity for a camera shot. Otherwise they plodded steadily. After two hours the conviction was rapidly growing in the mind of everyone, save Temberly, that Venus was a remarkably dull place.

'Just a damned great forest of celery,' observed Heerdahl. 'I say, Tem,' he shouted up the line, 'why is all this stuff so corpse-like?'

'I don't know – been wondering about it. Obviously these plants have no chlorophyll; they must use something else instead. It may be that they don't break down carbon dioxide the same way, or perhaps they don't use it at all. I can't tell you anything about them until I've had a chance to do a few experiments.'

The party continued its advance in silence. There was a sudden shout and an explosion ahead.

'What is it?'

'Missed it,' said Bill's voice disgustedly. 'Little thing a bit bigger than a rabbit – same colour as everything else in this rotten world.'

'A mammal?' enquired Temberly excitedly.

'How the devil should I know – I only caught a glimpse of it running. Anyhow, it shows that there is something besides plants in the miserable place.'

He called back down the line a few minutes later.

'I say, it seems to be getting clearer out there on the right. What about making that way?'

'You're leading.'

They came out at the head of a shallow dip of land leading down to the shore of a large stretch of water. Whether sea or lake, it was difficult to tell. The limit of visibility being always low on Venus, the water appeared to stretch away until it indefinably mixed with the hanging mist. Hal tasted the water and was just opening his mouth to pronounce it fresh, when away on the left came the sound of a long rumbling bellow, followed by that of a colossal splash.

Quick as a flash, Crawshaw had unslung his rifle and torn off over the adjoining rise in the direction of the noise, leaving the rest unrecovered from their alarm of the unearthly roar.

'Damn the man,' said Hal. 'I'll go and fetch him back. You look after the others, Heerdahl.'

'What do you think that can have been?' Vida asked, watching her husband disappear in the wake of Crawshaw.

'God only knows,' Heerdahl said. 'There's no reasoning to go on in this place – might have been anything from one of those obsolete reptiles he talked about, to a factory hooter. Beastly mournful whatever it was.'

'Don't you think we ought to go too?'

'No, we might easily miss them. Besides, orders are orders. I think we might have a cigarette and pollute the air of Venus for the first time with tobacco smoke.'

The two sat down and leaned back against a rock. Heerdahl put his rifle across his knees, lit Vida's cigarette and then his own. He inhaled deeply and with satisfaction.

'That's good.'

Temberly had wandered down to the water's edge and was busily filling little vials and packing them in his specimen case for future examination. He then bent down to examine some subwater growths with a deep attention which rendered it possible to consider him safe for the moment. Freda was indefatigably brandishing her camera at a variety of likely and unlikely objects.

'You know,' Heerdahl reflected, 'this might be quite a pleasant world if only it didn't look so drearily monotonous. I don't think I ever realised before what a difference colour can make.'

Vida nodded.

'It's rather like living in a photograph – nothing but whites and greys and darker greys. With this diffused light there aren't even any clear-cut shadows.'

'Not much use for sundials in this place – I wonder if the sun does ever truly shine? By the way, how long is it since we left the *Fyra*?'

'About three hours.'

'Then I should think we'll have a fair spell of daylight yet. We'd only just left the shadow when we landed, so it was not very long after dawn. Hullo, what's Tom up to?'

Temberly was knee-deep in the water looking agitatedly down and pouncing from time to time, apparently without making any catch.

'What is it?' Heerdahl called.

'Fish – come and look at them.'

'Oh, hang fish. I prefer to be comfortable.'

He and Vida continued a desultory conversation during the following half hour. No further bellow broke the silence, though once or twice big ripples on the surface of the water gave an indication of unknown creatures stirring in the depths.

'I hope they're both all right,' Vida said nervously.

'Oh, they know how to look after themselves, besides we'd have heard shots if there had been any trouble.'

Even as Heerdahl finished speaking, a hail reached them as they saw two figures striding over the skyline.

'Nothing,' said Crawshaw with deep disgust, in answer to their enquiries. 'We poked around a bit and found footprints the size of dining tables leading down to the water, but we never got a smell of the creature itself.'

'No need to be so gloomy. You could scarcely have carried the thing home if you had shot it,' Heerdahl pointed out.

Temberly left his dabbling and walked up to the party.

'Most interesting,' he announced. 'A three-eyed fish. One eye set in the top of its head. Of course there were such things on Earth, but I never hoped to see more than a vestigial third eye, at best. This is a very interesting place, you know.'

'Glad you think so,' grunted Crawshaw. He turned to Heerdahl.

'Where's Freda got to?'

They all looked around. There was no sign of Freda.

Crawshaw turned glaring upon Heerdahl.

'You were left in charge here – why did you let her go? It was your business to look after her.'

Heerdahl coloured angrily.

'Protection was my job and I'd have done it if it had been necessary. I wasn't told to be a nursemaid. I couldn't keep the girl here by force.'

'You ought to have forbidden her to go out of sight.'

'A lot of notice she'd have taken of orders from me – or from anyone else.'

'Shut up, you two,' said Hal. 'You won't get anywhere by reviling one another. Bill, you've got a voice like a foghorn. Let it go.'

Bill obeyed with a stentorian bellow which, in the thick air, sounded very little inferior to a foghorn. They listened tensely for a reply and Vida thought she heard a faint answering hail on the right. Heerdahl agreed.

'Anyhow, she must have gone in that direction. If she went back into the forest the way we came, Vida and I would have seen her, and if she'd gone along the shore to the left you two would have met her.'

Hal nodded.

'We'd better get along. We can leave signs marking our way so that she can follow on if we miss her. Now, for God's sake, everybody keep together this time.'

Their way along the waterside was easy. The main forest did not begin within some hundred yards of the brink and left a walking surface covered only with the usual matted tendrils. Visibility, however, was rendered poorer than ever by the constant undulations of the land. Hal Newton has recorded that for the atmosphere to be so dry and clear as to allow sight of even a large object more than a mile away, is a rare occurrence indeed on Venus.

At intervals Crawshaw emitted another powerful shout and the party paused to listen vainly.

'Heaven knows what she wanted to come along here for,' he grumbled, 'it's all just the same as the place we stopped at.'

'FREDA!' he bawled again.

This time there came an unmistakable answering shout from somewhere ahead. The whole party took to its heels.

'Just over the next rise, I should think,' Hal said jerkily as they pelted down the side of a shallow gully.

They reached the next vantage point and paused, breathing heavily, to look about.

Some three or four hundred yards ahead they could make out the figure of Freda. Her head was bent over her inevitable camera, while around her clustered a group of some eight or nine pigmy creatures.

'Put that up you fool,' snapped Crawshaw to Heerdahl. 'You can't use a rocket-shell rifle at this range – you'd blow the whole lot of them to bits. Besides we'd have heard her pistol if they had attacked her.'

'The best thing we can do is to get in close quietly, we don't want to scare the things and spoil her chances of a good photograph,' advised Hal.

'I say, did you see that?' Vida asked.

'What?'

'I did – she spoke to them,' Heerdahl said.

'Don't be a fool,' Crawshaw began. 'How the blazes – ?'

'Hands up,' called a high-pitched voice behind them.

VI

DINGTONS AND WOTS

The five swung round.

'What the – ?'

'Hands up,' demanded the voice.

At the sight of six levelled barrels they obeyed swiftly. Then followed a silence as the explorers gazed amazedly at their captors. The holders of the insistent weapons returned the stares unblinkingly.

They bore more resemblance, perhaps, to monkeys than to any other earthly form of animal, yet the likeness was remote. For one thing, they stood upright with the straightness of man though their legs were very short in proportion to the rest of the body. For another, the close, silvery grey hair which covered them, grew even on their faces. The average height must have been somewhere between four feet four inches and four feet six, and their heads showed evidence of no mean mental development.

The faces of the creatures were given an oddly half-human look by reason of their high-bridged noses. And the hands, with thumbs set in opposition, differed from the human hand only in possessing a curved claw at the end of each finger.

Six of these claws were hooked menacingly round the triggers of six weapons.

Crawshaw broke the silence, and with it, the spell of indecision which seemed to hold both parties.

'Did – did they speak in English?' he asked incredulously.

Hal wore a puzzled frown.

'It certainly seemed that way,' he admitted, 'but – hang it, it must be a form of mental suggestion. We only thought we heard the actual words when they transmitted the thought. They couldn't – '

As though to contradict Hal's theory, one of the creatures spoke and they could see its lips form the words.

'Take their guns,' it said.

A companion laid his rifle carefully on the ground and approached. Crawshaw lowered one hand threateningly.

'Stop it, Bill. Do you want to get us all killed? We better submit gracefully for the moment – they've got the drop on us now.'

The creature relieved them of all their pistols and rocket-shell rifles, looked doubtfully for a moment at Hal's radio transmitter and, intent on taking no chances, removed that as well with the air of one who is going to be on the safe side. He handed the haul to his companions who regarded them curiously before slinging them to their own trappings.

'Look out,' Heerdahl called involuntarily as the leader fingered a rocket-rifle trigger in a meditative fashion.

The creature looked up at him solemnly for a moment, then nodded and resumed his examination of the mechanism. He appeared puzzled by the rocket-shell cartridges, though he accorded the bullet cartridges of the pistols a barely interested glance; evidently the former were new to him. At length he too slung the rifle on his back and advanced to peer closely into the faces of the captives. Again he seemed puzzled, but whatever his problem was he decided it could wait until later and turned to give an order to his followers. The whole party moved off from the rise towards the spot where Freda was still to be seen plying her camera.

'Well, I'll say that girl's got the reporter's mind right enough – that's the spirit which made the front page what it is today,' Heerdahl said admiringly.

As they approached, Freda broke off an animated conversation to greet them.

'Hullo,' she said. 'I hoped you'd be along soon.'

'Well of all the –' Crawshaw began.

'Very kind of you,' Hal remarked coldly. 'May I ask what the devil you think we're going to do now?'

Freda shook her head.

'The question more properly is – what is going to be done with us? And there seems to be rather a difference of opinion about that. It all depends apparently whether we are Dingtons or Wots.'

'Whether we're what or what?'

'No. Whether we're Dingtons or Wots.'

'Or – ?'

'Don't you understand? They want to know whether you are a Dington, or whether you are a Wot.'

'Oh, I see. Well, what are they, anyway?'

'That's just what I'm trying to find out.'

Freda turned back to her group of the creatures and resumed conversation. Hal rumpled his hair and scratched his head thoughtfully. As far as could be judged, the grey animals intended no harm. They seemed a placid and unexcitable breed, but on the other hand they carried weapons, and their first act had been to disarm himself and his party. At the moment there seemed to be no desire to make a move of any kind, all attention was concentrated on Freda and her conversation. Her conversation, that was the wildest improbability since they had landed.

'Hang it all,' Hal murmured, 'it's a bit steep. We come across twenty-five million miles of space – more than that – and what happens? The first inhabitants we meet on a strange planet address us in English. Damn it all, something's wrong somewhere.'

He turned to the leader of the guards in an attempt to clear up the anomaly and listened closely as the creature tried to reply to his question. Despite the unusual pitch and hardness of tone in the voice, he was able to detect the presence of an unfamiliar accent and of other slight differences. His enquiry was misunderstood. Apparently the word 'English' conveyed no meaning to the other though he spoke the language itself. Hal reshuffled his thoughts and tried another start. He indicated the members of his party.

'We are men – what are you?'

'Gorlaks,' replied the creature promptly and then added: 'Are you Dingtons or Wots?'

'Oh, damn,' said Hal.

Temberly from the first had been observing the Gorlaks with the closest attention.

'Look,' he said, pointing to the furry grey figure to which Freda was talking. They followed the line of his finger.

From a kind of pocket in the creature's front protruded the doll-like head of a miniature Gorlak whose bright little eyes were following their movements with solemn interest.

'Oh, isn't it sweet?' said Vida advancing to the mother and her furry baby.

'Marsupials,' Temberly remarked half to himself.

The Gorlak leader's sharp ears overheard him. He shook his head.

'Monotremes,' he corrected proudly.

Temberly looked surprised and nodded thoughtfully.

'I know what a marsupial is, but I'm hanged if I've ever knowingly met a monotreme before. What is it?' Heerdahl asked.

'A step beyond reptiles. That is, it has warm blood and grows hair, but it still lays eggs and carries them in a pouch to hatch them out.'

'That sounds a pretty efficient sort of system.'

'So one would think, but for some reason or other monotremes never made great headway on Earth. We went on to the mammal stage and there are very few of this intermediate stage left. They seem to have taken well here and developed a high intelligence.'

He turned back to the Gorlak.

'Are there many kinds of monotremes?'

'Five.'

'And mammals, have you any of them?'

'Only Dingtons and Wots.'

'Oh, hang it all, can't somebody clear up this business?' groaned Heerdahl.

'Now, listen to me – ' he began but he got no further.

A plaintive sound on a high, carrying note came floating from the direction of the forest. Every Gorlak became suddenly alert.

'Dington,' said the Gorlak leader. He produced a curiously shaped whistle and blew on it to cause the same mournful note. In a few seconds came an answer, whereat the Gorlak blew again.

'Well, we look like finding out what a Dington is at last,' said Hal as they watched the forest expectantly.

Again the note sounded. It was evident that the creature, whatever it was, was approaching, for the sound was much louder. The Gorlaks burst for a moment into high-pitched conversation which was impossible to follow.

'Good heavens, it's a bird – Look there, just over the trees!' cried Crawshaw.

Something with slowly flapping wings of tremendous span was looming out of the mist.

'It's pretty low – only just clearing – Good Lord, that's no bird, it's a machine,' Hal gasped. 'An ornithopter, sure as I'm alive.'

They all stared at the leisurely-approaching craft.

'It's sinking too fast. It'll hit those trees as sure as – there, that bent it some.'

The plane had just failed to clear the last outpost of the forest. Its wing tips, at the bottom of their stroke, fouled the bushy heads of the white trees and the whole contraption was knocked into a forward somersault. For a moment it threshed furiously before coming to rest inverted and asprawl, among the lower bushes. Shrill cries of alarm arose from the Gorlaks; with one accord they rushed off in the direction of the capsized flier, leaving their prisoners to shift for themselves.

'Well, we'd better go, too, seeing that they've got all the weapons,' said Hal.

With the advantage of their longer legs they easily overtook the Gorlaks, and arrived well in the van at the wreckage. Somewhere in the jumble of broken wings and tangled bushes something was struggling. It evidently heard their approach.

'Hullo. Help me out of this damned thing, will you?' called an unmistakably human voice.

The aviator, when extracted, proved to be a tall, well-built man. A mop of fair hair surmounted a face which would have seemed remarkably pallid on Earth, but all were now growing so used to the grey-whites of Venus that they were able to make allowances for it. There was a twinkle of amusement in his eyes as he looked from one to another of their astounded faces and his mouth twisted with a smile as he spoke.

'You've been a long time,' he said, 'but you are very welcome.'

There seemed no possible reply to this remark, and they remained silently surprised. The man seemed more amused than before. He turned to the leader of the Gorlaks.

'*Arrul*. Get us some food.'

Several of the Gorlaks scurried around and began to pull up neighbouring plants. As they laid the bulbous roots before the party, the flying man picked one up and offered it to Vida, indicating that the rest should help themselves.

'You will find these quite good, though perhaps not very tasty,' he suggested. 'Explanations are so much easier when one is reinforced with a meal, and I haven't had anything to eat since before dawn.'

The rest picked up the vegetables. The flavour was weak, but they were not unpleasant, and a good cure for growing hunger.

VII

ATTACK!

The guard of four aboard the *Fyra* was finding time hanging heavy on its hands. They had all watched the rest of the crew disappear into the forest, with mixed feelings. In Lucy a definite sense of misgiving arose. She had been startled to see Temberly's misadventure with the strange Venusian flower and, though it had luckily turned out to be nothing more than a cause for laughter at his expense, it seemed to her to hint of mysterious dangers.

It was with uncomfortable apprehension, therefore, that she saw the forest swallow them up. Whether this had its root cause in a fear for them, and Temberly with them, or in a feeling that the four in the *Fyra* were now marooned in this strange place, she could not tell. She turned to Smith, at her side.

'It would have been better if they had left Heerdahl with us. Suppose they are gone a long time or get into some kind of difficulties, we can't take the ship to look for them.'

Smith nodded agreement. He, too, was feeling depressed.

'Yes, we ought to have had a spare pilot – though Mackay might be able to move the ship if it should come to a pinch.'

For the next two hours or so they occupied themselves about the *Fyra* in cleaning up the cabins and making ship-shape after the inevitable disorders of the run. Lucy, with her characteristic appearance of having allowed her thoughts to wander far away from her surroundings, was straightening out the chaotic condition of the pantry when Smith's voice recalled her to the window.

'I say,' he shouted excitedly, 'come and look here.'

Mackay and Freeman also crowded close to the fused panes. 'What is it?'

For answer, Smith pointed silently at the edge of the forest. The spot he indicated was further away than that at which the others had disappeared and, consequently less distinct. Through the misty air they could dimly make out a white figure moving slowly towards them – without doubt a biped.

They offered no comment as they watched it approach. At last it came to a range at which it was clearly visible as a man. He paused for a while in interested contemplation of the ship. It was obvious that he had not yet seen the watchers in the windows and they were granted a good chance of observing him.

He stood a little less than six feet, as nearly as could be judged. His head was covered with thick, black hair which fell in a tangled mass about his shoulders. A beard, no less unkempt, straggled down across his chest. The only attempt at clothing was a short kilt of woven, whitish cloth and a broad belt to secure it. To the belt were attached a number of small pouches and a few hooks from which implements dangled. In the crook of one arm rested unmistakably a rifle.

The four looked at one another in surprise. Of the many

126

things they had been prepared to meet, man had been one of the least expected.

The figure moved out of their field of vision, still regarding the ship intently.

'Gone around to starboard,' announced Mackay.

'Is the entrance port closed?' Smith enquired nervously.

Freeman set off to meet the visitor, or to close the port should it seem necessary, while the rest moved over to the starboard windows for a view of the encounter. The result was disappointing. The prowler's jaw dropped for a second, then he turned and scuttled for cover like a rabbit.

'Queer,' remarked Lucy. 'Did you notice that he was white all over, like everything else here?'

Freeman returned.

'Guess he didn't like my face. Wasn't long in making up his mind, either. What happened to him?'

'Went back round the bow and streaked for the forest,' Mackay replied.

'I suppose you've closed the port?' asked Smith.

Freeman looked at him.

'Sure, I closed it. Though it hardly seems necessary when the natives are as frightened as mice. What are you scared about, anyway?'

Smith shifted uncomfortably.

'I – I don't know. I reckon the whole damned place looks pretty nasty to me. I wouldn't care so much if something would happen; it's all this hanging fire feeling that I don't like.'

He looked ashamed of himself, but brightened as Lucy backed him up.

'I know just how you feel. This place affects me the same way,' she said.

The two engineers returned to their interrupted work and Lucy to her pantry while Smith kept watch at the window for a possible reappearance of the native. It was almost an hour later when he called to the other again.

'He's coming back. Seems to be beckoning or something of the sort.'

'Yes, he's beckoning,' Mackay agreed. 'I wonder why this sudden change of front – he wasn't too keen on us before?'

'After all, one would expect a savage to be scared at first,' Lucy pointed out.

'Not too much of the savage about him. That looked like a fairly useful gun to me.'

Mackay turned an enquiring look on Freeman.

'Well, what about it?'

'Sure, I'm game,' Freeman agreed. 'We'll just take pistols – you two cover us with rocket-rifles,' he instructed Lucy and Smith.

The two men set out side by side across the squashing growths, towards the beckoner. They signed to him to advance and meet them, but he appeared to prefer his own choice of ground. Half the distance from the ship had been covered when the man slid back into the foliage.

'What the – ?' Mackay began, but his question was answered before it was expressed.

The sharp crack of an explosion reached them. Simultaneously Freeman dropped.

Mackay hit the ground a split-second later. The rapidity of his taking cover tokened an adventurous life.

'Blast him,' he muttered, but his words were drowned as the two on the *Fyra* sent replies crashing into the forest. The two rocket-shells exploded in the same flash among the trees.

'And that's settled him,' thought Mackay, but he was canny. He unbuckled the holster of his pistol and raised it above cover. A shot drilled it promptly. Again there came the crash of rocket-shells as the ship answered.

Mackay crawled over to Freeman and inspected the wound with some relief. The bullet had just flicked him lightly, enough to stun and to draw a trickle of blood, but the most serious result would probably be a bad headache for a while. He grasped the other by one leg and started to crawl back, towing him towards the ship. Bullets still whistled over his head from the forest, and crashes behind him told that Lucy and Smith were returning the fire with interest. Gradually the attackers slackened and ceased, but Mackay was taking no risks. He crawled until he was near the spot where he must rise to climb aboard the *Fyra*.

'Give them hell while I make a bolt for it,' he called up to the pair.

Under cover of a furious burst of rocket-shells, he stood up with Freeman across his shoulders, tipped the other into the entrance port and climbed in himself. The door closed with a thud as Smith pulled over the control.

Lucy put up her rifle and went in search of water and bandages while Mackay, over the insensible form of his friend, made unprintable remarks about the Venusian natives and their ancestors.

'Well, thank God the – fools hadn't got the sense to wait until we were closer,' he ended.

Under Lucy's ministrations, Freeman soon came to. He lifted one hand to his head, simultaneously producing a flood of language which rivalled Mackay's outburst, then:

'Did you get him?' he asked.

'Him?' said Smith. 'There must have been dozens of the devils. We blew the part where the one man vanished into little bits and then churned up the stuff for a good few yards on either side. But they're at it again. Listen.'

Through the thick armour of the *Fyra* an intermittent tapping was audible.

'Bullets.'

Mackay smiled slightly.

'Let 'em waste the stuff. A peashooter would be as useful to them – and just as effective against this bus. Let 'em try rocket-shells if they like.'

Smith crossed to one of the windows and called back:

'They're advancing. A whole big ring of them closing in. Several hundred of them, I'd guess.'

'I suppose they think that they're safe now that we've shut the entrance,' Mackay growled. 'The irritating thing is that they're damn well right – our windows aren't made to open, and we can't do a thing but sit here like sardines in a can.'

Freeman, almost recovered now, looked up with a grin.

'We can give them a nasty jolt when they come closer.'

He stood up and swayed a little uncertainly before staggering off forward in the direction of the controls.

'What's his little game?' Smith asked.

Mackay gave a broad smile.

'Come and see,' he replied, motioning them to the window.

At their appearance a spatter of lead rained against the fused glass. Lucy started back in alarm.

'It's all right,' Mackay advised. 'This stuff beats six-inch steel.'

The crowd was now clustered closely round the ship. They could see the pale men's mouths opening and shutting and knew that they were shouting as they brandished their weapons. Some were even battering on the hull with rifle butts, though not a sound was audible inside, save the occasional flick of a bullet.

'Watch,' said Mackay.

The ship trembled slightly as there came a growling rumble. From fore and aft sprang sudden belches of flame, while a line of fire ran spurting swiftly down each side. The enemy broke and ran to a respectful distance.

'He turned the rockets on them. First the main driving and braking bunches, then a flip on the side steering tubes,' explained Mackay. 'I guess he was feeling sore about that bullet he turned.'

'And now?' asked Lucy.

Mackay shrugged his shoulders.

'Checkmate. We just wait for something to happen.'

The enemy's reaction to the situation was similar. A number detached themselves to fetch food from the forest and then all settled down comfortably – though well out of range of the rocket tube flames.

Freeman came back looking worried.

'We don't want the others to run into this gang when they come back. Can't you get them a warning on the radio, Smith?'

'I've tried. Couldn't raise a chirp from them. I guess Hal's set must have packed up or something.'

A few minutes later, an unusual glitter caught Lucy's eye. She pointed:

'Look. There's something flashing among the trees.'

VIII

EXPLANATION

The fair-haired young man looked around the group.

'Permit me,' he said, 'to introduce myself – Knight Dington.'

Hal briefly introduced his party and himself.

'Now would you be so kind as to explain a few of these anomalies?' he suggested.

'Such as – ?'

'Well, how you come to be speaking English, for instance, and the nature of all this Dington and Wot business.'

'Then you didn't know?'

'Didn't know what?'

'Why, that we were here.'

'Look here, suppose we start this thing at the beginning,' Crawshaw interrupted. 'Now, how is it that you and these – er – Gorlaks, speak English?'

'Because, apart from the Gorlaks' own peculiar language, it is the only one known on Venus,' Knight replied with a mischievous twinkle. 'But I'll try to explain. I suppose you have heard of Noah Watson's *Ark*?'

'You mean to say that the *Ark* really – ?'

'Yes. In spite of the jeers it caused, it achieved its purpose. It left the Earth and landed on Venus.'

'Then you are – ?'

'I'll try to make it short. In the *Ark*, as you probably know, there were roughly one hundred and twenty persons – it was a large machine. Now, Noah Watson and Henry Headington were two men whose principles were vitally opposed. They agreed, in fact, about only one thing, and that was the imminent destruction of the Earth – a matter in which they were both entirely wrong.

'Headington soon found out that he had been misguided, but Watson to the end would never admit that he had been wrong. Headington looked back from space at the world from which he had exiled himself, and cursed because there was no turning back. From that moment he began to hate Watson. And Watson, still convinced that the Earth was now barren, unveiled the dislike he had hitherto concealed for Headington's way of life.

'By the time they reached Venus, it was quite clear that they would never co-operate to build up a new civilisation. They separated the moment they could leave the ship and never saw one another again.

'The *Ark* made a very rough landing. Only some seventy-two of the passengers survived it. Of these, thirty followed Headington, while the other forty attached themselves to Watson. The two parties, with enmity in their hearts, set off in opposite directions and founded communities according to their different lights.

131

'All this, as you know, took place nearly 800 Earth years ago – about 1298 Venusian years – plenty of time to build nations where food grows readily to hand.

'Our records tell us that in the course of time various modifications have occurred. Our skins have lost their pigmentation and our chests are a little smaller since lung capacity does not need to be as great. Our muscular strength, on the other hand, has remained at an approximately constant average since the pull of gravity is only a trifle less.

'The language has undergone merely a few, very slight changes in colloquialisms and metaphors, mostly derived from the names we were forced to coin to describe phenomena peculiar to Venus. Otherwise we believe we have changed very little.'

'Then your nations are – ?' Hal began.

'They are named after their leaders. Headington gradually became contracted to Dington in popular speech, just as Watson became Wot. I, myself, claim direct descent from the original Henry Headington, but the surname, too, has become Dington.

'The things which most puzzled Arrul and the other Gorlaks, when they found you, was really your complexions. Although the fact that you are fully-clad pointed to your being Dingtons, yet you were not normal Dingtons, but neither did you look like Wots. They can never have really thought you were Wots, or you would not be alive now.'

Knight looked at their faces again and smiled.

'You will excuse me,' he said, 'but no wonder the poor Gorlaks were worried. You see, except when fashion decrees it for some of our women, coloured faces are unknown here.'

Vida looked curiously at the young man.

'You didn't seem very surprised at seeing us,' she remarked.

'I was searching for you.'

'But how did you know – ?'

'An Earth ship was bound to come sooner or later. Once the secret of space travel had been solved, it was certain to be rediscovered. The thing which most surprises us is that you have been so long in coming. From the first, old Henry Headington used to gaze up at the clouds which hid the stars and the Earth he loved so well, saying that soon you would come and rescue him. But the months drew into years and the years

132

into centuries, and so, for eight hundred years we have watched and waited, though no longer from any desire to be rescued.'

Vida felt a surge of pity for the poor old man, far back in the past, watching the rolling clouds for the help which never came. Knight's voice was continuing:

'Last night we heard the roar of rockets and saw the red glow in the sky. There was an uproar and shouting; all the cities went wild. Everyone knew that the old man's faith was upheld at last. But you passed over us, heading into the Wot country. As soon as it became light – it was almost dawn when you passed – we sent out a fleet of scouts to find you.'

They had risen to their feet during the last few sentences, and were preparing to depart.

'Can we go straight to your ship?' Knight enquired eagerly.

Hal nodded and produced from his pocket a small instrument in which a needle swung. The Dington looked at it curiously.

'I've heard of that. A compass, isn't it? I'm afraid it's no good here.'

'No,' said Hal, 'I tried a compass before we set out and found that it just idled. This little thing is specially built so that it is always attracted to the ship.'

He steadied it for a moment. Then they turned their backs on the lake and plunged into the forest in the direction indicated by the needle. Knight hung back a moment and applied a light to the crumpled remains of his ornithopter. As the machine went up in a sheet of flame he came running after the rest.

'Doesn't do to let Wots get hold of them,' he explained.

Less than two miles had been covered when distant crashes became audible ahead.

'Rocket shells,' said Crawshaw. 'Rifle size, I'd judge.'

'What are they?' asked Knight.

Hal briefly explained the principle of the self-propelling, explosive bullet.

'Never heard of them,' Knight assured him.

'Then it must be our folks. Let's get a move on.'

A while later there came a short, thunderous blast from the *Fyra*'s driving rockets.

'What on earth – ? Anyway, they can't have moved her,' Hal added, after waiting in vain for a repetition of the sound.

Half an hour later they came suddenly to the edge of the clearing. An exclamation broke from Knight, and he motioned the party back with one hand.

'Look there,' he said.

They gazed in consternation at the shaggy headed, half-nude crowd surrounding the *Fyra.*

'Wots,' said Knight in answer to their unspoken question. 'This is going to be difficult.'

'There must be hundreds of them. We can't attack that lot. How are they armed?'

'Rifles – they always carry them. Although their motto is "What's natural's right", they unfortunately make an exception in the matter of rifles – they're pretty fine shots, too. Though, even unarmed, they'd tear you to bits.'

'But we don't want to hurt them,' Vida objected.

'Doubtless, but you don't understand these people; they are fanatics – dangerous fanatics. If they got hold of you – '

Bill Crawshaw interrupted rudely. His trigger finger was itching.

'This isn't any time for lectures. What are we going to do?'

'You better tell your people to sit tight where they are if you've got any means of getting a message through,' Knight suggested.

Hal took his radio transmitter from the Gorlak who still carried it. Everyone watched as he tried for connection.

'No good. Can't raise them although there's a wire out.'

He thought for a moment.

'I suppose nobody's got a lamp?'

'I have,' said Heerdahl unexpectedly.

'Good man, that's lucky. A heliograph's no good in this diffused light. Smith knows Morse, he used to be on telegraphs.' He slipped the torch into a pocket and turned to one of the white trees.

'Don't go higher than about ten feet. These don't stand much weight,' Knight advised.

For a few moments there was no reply, then an answering flash appeared in the *Fyra*'s window.

'All safe?' Hal flashed.

'All O.K.'

'Those men outside are really dangerous.'

'We've had some.'

'Then keep where you are. Don't open port until we have

134

driven them off. Going for help now.'

'O.K.'

Either the exchange of messages had been unobserved by
the Wots, or else, as seemed more likely, they had not realised
that the ship's flashes were anything more than accidental. Hal
descended and handed the lamp back to Heerdahl.

'What now?' he asked Knight.

'We've got to rouse Chicago and get them on the job.'

'I beg your pardon?'

Knight grinned.

'I suppose it does sound a bit strange to you. You see, old
man Headington came from a place of that name, on Earth,
so he chose to call our main city after it for old time's sake – he
thought it sounded homely.'

'Lead on. Now that I know the others are safe, I'm all for
seeing your idea of Chicago.'

IX

AMBUSH

Temberly plucked at Hal's arm, his face was white with anxiety
and his eyes pleaded for reassurance as he asked:

'You're sure they'll be all right, Hal? I mean, Lucy's in
there and if anything should happen to her – ' He left the
sentence uncompleted.

'They'll be all right, old man. They're as safe there as any
place in the universe. I'll bet a twelve-inch rocket shell would
only dent the *Fyra*.'

'Yes, of course,' said Temberly. 'I thought so, it's only –
well, you know.'

'I know.'

A hoarse, sawing kind of whisper came from Crawshaw.

'Freda, for God's sake, come back. We're going now.'

Freda, who had wriggled forward to the very edge of the
clearing, stopped her camera, sighed and came squirming back
to them.

'Lucky I brought a telephoto lens – it's a pretty long shot, and about the worst possible kind of light. Still, I think I've got it here,' she said calmly, patting her camera.

'You'll drive me grey,' said Crawshaw. 'You little devil, how many times have I told you – ?'

'Now, Bill dear, don't be a bear. You know perfectly well that I will not be ordered – '

'Come on,' said Knight. 'The sooner we get away, the better. It's not healthy here. Arrul is leaving five of his Gorlaks to watch. He and the rest are coming with us. He's given orders that one of them is to overtake us and report if anything seems to be moving here.'

The procession took up its march while the Gorlaks who were to remain slid among the bushes. They seemed to disappear almost uncannily, so like was their colour to that of their surroundings.

Knight led them in silence through the monotonous forest with a sureness and lack of hesitation which puzzled Hal. At last he enquired how it was done. Knight looked surprised.

'That's odd. I never thought of it. I just know which is the general direction of Chicago – that's all.'

'But how?'

'Sort of instinct. You use a compass on Earth, but as it doesn't work here, I suppose we've subconsciously developed a high sense of direction. But even if I were wrong, Arrul would tell us. Gorlaks always seem to know where they are.'

As they trudged on, Hal put another question on a subject yet unexplained.

'We expected to find this world teeming with primitive monsters. So far we've only heard one, and seen a number of little, rabbit-sized creatures. Aren't there many big reptiles?'

'According to history, there were plenty, but they've mostly been killed by us or by the Wots. You see, rifles can do a lot in eight hundred years. A land reptile, that is, a large land reptile, is rare now, but there are plenty of weird things in the seas and rivers. That's been one of our greatest stumbling blocks. We think it probable that, although there is a great deal of water, there is more land than the continent we know, but we can't find out for certain.'

'But surely, in all this time – '

'Think of our conditions. Nobody has yet managed to make a ship able to withstand the bigger marine monsters. If such a ship were built, there would then be the fuel problem. Such coal as we have is, geologically speaking, very recent and very poor, at that. On Earth you are said to have hard wood which burns well, but all our vegetation is soft, with a high percentage of water. Some of us have been drilling for combustible oil, but we have found none. It is no good depending on wind, for there seldom is more than a breath stirring.

'We have been able to manage a compact storage battery for our planes and other purposes, but it is no good for long-distance work. Besides, even in this continent there are some parts where planes are attacked by *pteranodons*, almost as big as the machines themselves – even the *pterodactyl*, which is comparatively small, is likely to wreck a plane if it should fly at it. Luckily they have learned to avoid these parts.'

'What a happy planet,' remarked Heerdahl, who had joined them. 'But the things which really get me are how and why you use ornithopters – we were never able to do anything with them on Earth?'

'Oh, that's easy. None of our ground is clear for take-off or landing, what's more we can keep very little of it clear if we try. It's always like this again if left for a few days.' Knight kicked a bunch of tangled white growths. 'The water's out of the question for a plane, as it is for a ship. So that killed the idea of a screw-driven plane. None of our chemists has been successful in duplicating the explosives which drove the *Ark*, and the only men who knew the secret were killed when the ship landed. So that puts rockets out. The only thing to do was to evolve something which would cope with both our conditions and limitations.'

'But the lift?'

'You must remember the denseness of our atmosphere, and the way design advances when concentrated upon.'

Heerdahl nodded.

'I'd like to examine one of these machines of yours.'

'You'll have a chance soon.'

Vida had been looking worried ever since they had left the clearing. Now, with a quick glance round to see that none of the Gorlaks was within hearing, she asked:

'Are you sure that it was quite safe to leave the Gorlaks to watch?'

'Safe?' Knight looked puzzled.

'I mean are they quite trustworthy? There's no chance, for

137

instance, of them giving warning to the Wots that we are here?'

For a moment Knight looked indignant at the questioning of the little creatures' loyalty. Then he remembered that Vida could not be expected to understand.

'The Gorlaks are our friends,' he said with slight reproof in his voice. 'They keep well away from Wots, in fact we gave them rifles to shoot Wots.'

'You gave them rifles to use against your own kind?' Vida asked incredulously. 'Why?'

'Partly because Gorlaks are a delicacy to Wots.'

'You don't mean – ?'

'Yes, they eat them.'

Vida's eyes widened with surprise and horror. Instinctively, she looked back along the line to the mother Gorlak and that little furry-headed baby which regarded the world so solemnly. She shuddered and felt suddenly sick.

'No,' she said. Heerdahl burst in.

'But they're – they're – good heavens man, it's almost cannibalism.'

'That's how we look at it,' Knight nodded. 'The Wots, however – '

A high pitched cry in the rear cut him short and brought the party to a halt. Arrul came up the line, bringing with him a Gorlak who panted heavily.

'What is it?' Knight asked.

The messenger reported that about fifty of the Wots had left the clearing where the ship lay, and made off into the forest.

'Following us?'

No, the Gorlak said. They were away on the left somewhere, but he had thought it better to report.

'Quite right,' Knight agreed. He considered for a moment. 'I don't suppose it means anything but, Arrul, you might scatter your folks and keep a lookout.'

'Gorlaks,' he remarked as the march was resumed, 'are wonders for not being seen. They'll find out what is happening, all right.'

'You were talking about the Wots,' Heerdahl prompted.

'It is difficult to explain them without delivering a lecture,' said Knight. 'You see, so many causes have combined to make them as they are. Firstly, you must remember that they are descended from a fanatic or the close followers of a fanatic. It is even probable that Watson became thoroughly unhinged towards the end. He certainly compiled a remarkable book which seems to consist in part of an old work called the Bible, but mostly of his own instructions and prophecies.

'The Wots have so based their customs upon him, that in the course of time the teaching of Watson, himself, has become more important to them than the earlier part of the book. I have heard some of our scholars say that as Moses was to the Israelites so is Watson to the Wots – that conveys little to me but, perhaps, more to you.'

'You mean that they almost worship him?'

'Some of them go further than that. There are figures and shrines set up to him in many places.'

'But their attitude to the Gorlaks?' asked Vida.

'That is an outcome of Watson's teaching. He might not have approved of their manner of treating the Gorlaks, but he wrote that man is the supreme work of God, and is the only possessor of a soul – therefore the Gorlaks are considered to be animals just as much as any of the reptiles. The slaughtering of the little grey people has become almost a point of honour with the Wots – a sort of defence of their own status.'

'That sounds like a kind of logical madness.'

'It is. You see, not only do they practice natural birth and disallow incubation, but in the absence of any food problem or any form of control, they have been able to breed promiscuously and at random – with some queer results. While we Dingtons realised that breeding, in such a small community, must be carefully watched so that no one strain will become over-emphasised, the Wots took no such care.

'Inbreeding is not harmful provided that the stock is well-matched, but among them the strain of Watson's mania – and possibly that of several of his followers – was allowed to run riot. The result is that the unstable and fanatical race of Wots is more than twice as numerous as our carefully-raised nation of Dingtons. We are beginning to be faced with a number of very grave problems.'

'So the Wots really went native.'

Knight looked puzzled; the phrase was evidently unfamiliar to him. Hal explained:

'I mean that we have a similar problem, though a small one, on Earth. In the tropics we find that a white man either conquers the conditions, or is conquered by them. It would seem, from what you say, that the Dingtons have conquered Venusian conditions, while the Wots have been beaten by them.'

'That just fits it,' Knight agreed. 'Except that you flatter the Dingtons. We still have an uphill fight.'

'What I can't understand about these Wot people,' interposed Crawshaw, 'is why the devil they want to attack us. We arrive on a perfectly friendly visit, and the first thing they do is to lay siege to our ship. Why?'

'Just because you are blasphemers.'

'We are?'

'Watson told his lot that the Earth was destroyed – they've always hated us because we said it was not. Now you have turned up and, from their point of view, you are a set of living blasphemies.'

'But surely – well, hang it all, don't we prove that the Earth still does exist?'

'That annoys them all the more – you obviously have not had much to do with a fanatical religion. Its very strength is its own immense obstinacy. If they once admitted that you have really come from Earth, then all the doctrine of Watson would begin to totter.'

'But – '

'Look out,' Knight cried, in sudden alarm.

Hal checked immediately. There was a sweet flavour in his mouth and nose. He tried to speak but the words would not come. His head swam and he had a sense of horrible sickness. Dimly he was aware of a hand firmly gripping his arm.

x

THE WOTS' RUSE

Hal's first sensation when he opened his eyes was a splitting headache. He lay for a moment on his back, looking up through the pale branches. The sky was darkening, but still shot with vivid streaks of colour. Something stirred beside him and in a flash he remembered recent events. He sat up with a groan at the stabbing ache which the movement caused. At one side,

Knight crouched with his head in his hands, while on the other Arrul squatted, looking at them both with concern.

'Oh, Lord,' he muttered, putting both hands to his temples.

'It'll pass in a few minutes,' Knight's muffled voice assured him.

To Hal's astonishment, the prediction proved true. The ache lifted as suddenly and definitely as if an actual weight had been removed. He looked around for the rest of their party. No one else was in sight, and he turned anxiously upon the other.

'Where are they? What's happened?'

Knight looked at him miserably and shamefacedly.

'Wots,' he said. 'Arrul thinks that the large party of them which left the clearing, made a quick march and cut us off. He couldn't get back in time to give us any warning.'

'But why didn't they take us with the others?'

'Overlooked us. Arrul turned up at the last moment and dragged you into the scrub. I managed to stagger there as well, and he contrived to hide us both. Don't talk too loudly – there may be some of them still about.'

'But, man, they've got Vida, Temberly, all of them.'

'I know, but we can't help them if we get caught too.'

'What will they do with them?'

Knight shook his head. If he knew he was not going to tell.

'To think that I was caught with an old trick like that,' he said, with a mixture of disgust and remorse.

'Like what?'

For answer, the other pointed to a plant which grew close by. Hal could see that it was the same kind of Venusian flower which had earlier covered Temberly with pollen.

'They wedge the petals apart with a little rod and pour a kind of powder inside. Then, having attached a fine wire to the rod, they clear off to a safe distance either leaving the wire in the victim's path, or taking the loose end in their hands. The moment the wire is jerked the rod slips, and down comes the upper petal, puffing the powder out like a poison-gas cloud. Then they just come up and collect those who were near enough to breathe any of it, and tie them up before they have time to recover – it's a common Wot trick.'

The last of the light had almost gone. Knight turned to Arrul.

'Can you take us through the dark?'

The Gorlak nodded. He never spoke unnecessarily. Knight seemed a little cheered.

'With luck, we'll be in time. They won't have got the others to the clearing yet. Wots never travel by night – they'd have to use lights and that would make them too good a mark for the Gorlak snipers. If we can get somewhere and send Chicago a message, we ought to be well on the way by dawn.'

'I suppose they will be taking the others to the clearing?'

'It's an even bet. Let's get on.'

Led by the little Gorlak, they stumbled on through the dark forest.

Lucy, on the *Fyra*, spent an uneasy night. It had been decided that, since they were perfectly safe, the best course was to follow ordinary routine. Accordingly, after supper they retired to bed. She soon found that the prospect of sleep was remote, seeming momentarily to recede further. She tossed restlessly listening to the snores which drifted down the corridor from those two hardened campaigners, Mackay and Freeman. She envied them their power of detachment.

Her Madonna-like face bore wrinkles as she worried over the safety of the other party. The message flashed to Smith, '*Going for help now*,' had been so brief and uninformative. She wished it had told more, though, of course, there had been the risk that the besiegers might have noticed.

'Going where? And to get help from whom?' Lucy asked herself.

Several times she crept quietly from her cabin to the main living-room and peered out at the attackers. In the dim light she was able to see that they had not left their posts, but lay sleeping on the open ground. What were they waiting for? Surely they must realise that the *Fyra*'s stores could support those inside for weeks, if necessary. But, if it came to that, why should they be hostile at all? None of the crew had offered fight until attacked.

Once more she climbed back to her berth and this time, while her thoughts wandered off after Temberly and the others, sleep overtook her.

It was Smith who woke her in the morning.

'Come here,' he was whispering from the doorway.

'Go away while I get dressed,' she commanded. 'What is it?'

'It's the men outside. Come and watch them a bit.'

The half-naked savages were all awake now. Some had made off for the forest, presumably in search of food, others were obviously on guard duty, while still more amused themselves according to their lights. It was to a group of the latter that Smith pointed. He and the girl watched them in silence.

'What's wrong with 'em? Have you ever seen people behave like that before?'

Lucy turned her head away. She was feeling sickened and disgusted and her face showed it.

'Yes,' she said. 'Once. It was amongst the more dangerous patients in a mental home.'

Smith nodded.

'I wondered if that was it. But the queerest thing is that the others don't seem to take any notice of them. Do you suppose they're all mad?'

'Either that, or they are so used to it that they don't notice,' Lucy replied. With an effort, she had overcome her instinctive revulsion and was watching critically again. The two engineers entered the room and stood behind them.

'What is it?' Mackay asked. Lucy told him.

'By gosh, you're right,' he agreed after a few minutes' inspection. He gave a grimace of distaste; the normal man's first reaction.

'No good thinking of parleying with that lot,' he said decisively. 'We stay right here until the others bring along an army of keepers, or whatever it is they've gone to fetch.'

He turned away from the spectacle outside and shepherded the rest to the middle of the room.

'Now we are going to eat,' he announced. 'What shall it be for breakfast?'

'I don't think I –' Lucy began.

'Oh, yes, you are, young woman. You needn't think I'm going to let you be put off your food by a bunch of lunatics, not even if I have to stuff it into your mouth myself. Come along and see what there is in the larder.'

Under Mackay's spell of cheerfulness, they almost managed to forget the loose-lipped creatures and their unpleasant antics outside. By the end of the meal, they felt a great deal improved in spirits. Mackay asked:

'Now what are we going to do? We don't know when the rest will be back, so we might as well get on with something useful in the meantime. Now you, Lucy –'

Smith, who had drifted across to the window again, called back over his shoulder.

'Something's doing in the forest. There's a whole lot of these brutes streaking over there as fast as they can leg it, and there's another lot coming out to meet them.'

Lucy picked up the field glasses and joined him. She twisted the focusing screw for a moment, then the glasses fell clattering to the metal floor. She swayed and went suddenly pale.

'What the – ? Catch her, she's fainted!'

Mackay snatched up the fallen glasses.

'My God,' he said, 'they've got them!'

Nobody spoke for a moment.

'Hal's not there. Good man, Hal, he's dodged them. There's still a hope that he will be able to get help unless – ' He stopped abruptly as the possibility of a grimmer cause for Hal's absence struck him.

The advancing Wots brought their prisoners close to the ship and arranged them in a row before the window. All had their arms tied behind their backs and looked weary and dishevelled. Various of the Wots had proudly possessed themselves of the rocket-shell rifles and pistols, but the other accoutrements remained with their owners, even Freda's camera still being slung upon her side, and Crawshaw's machete dangling from his belt, tantalisingly out of reach of his bound hands.

Temberly, white-faced, looked up at them and raised his eyebrows enquiringly. Mackay caught his meaning and nodded, pointing behind him to where Lucy lay. Vida stood among the captors with a cool aloofness, while Heerdahl appeared to be testing the effect of a potent flow of rocket-service language. One of the Wots hit him a blow across the mouth, sending him staggering to his knees.

'Swine,' said Mackay under his breath.

'I don't like the looks of this,' Freeman murmured.

'You're right – it's pretty ugly.'

There was a pause while several of the Wots consulted. One pointed to the two women, but the rest shook their heads. Then Temberly appeared to catch their notice, and they nodded agreement to some plan. The little biologist was roughly pushed nearer the window while the rest of the prisoners were drawn aside. One of the Wots produced a length of thin cord, tied it into a loop, and placed it about Temberly's head. Mackay's

144

fists clenched whitely as he glared in futile helplessness.

'This is hell,' muttered Freeman.

The Wot slipped a short rod through the loop, and began to twist . . .

A sound which was half whimper and half scream startled the two engineers. They swung round to see Lucy rushing from the room.

'By heaven, she's right,' cried Mackay, 'we can't stand for that.'

He charged after the girl, catching up a machete as he passed.

'The Wots' ruse was successful,' Heerdahl told Hal afterwards. 'It was bound to be. Those four could not stay quietly inside the *Fyra* watching poor Temberly's eyes almost start from his head and seeing his face go livid with agony while the Wots gleefully tightened the cord. Crawshaw and I struggled like mad, but we couldn't do a thing other than tell the Wots what we thought of them. Yes, they got the others out of the ship, all right, but you ought to have seen them come.

'There was a big bunch of Wots waiting by the port, all ready to pounce – you could see them crouch for the spring as the door began to open. But they didn't know Mackay and Freeman – nor did we until then. Those two plunged out with heavy machetes whirling like wild buzz-saws. Man, it was astounding; they must have mowed down half the gang in the first rush, then a lot more Wots ran up to help.

'Mackay and Freeman stood back to back and hewed at the ring around them. I could see Mackay's face, and I'll never forget the way he grinned as he laid about him. Over his shoulder I could see Freeman's head bobbing about, bound with a white bandage – he wasn't doing too badly, either. None of the Wots dared to try a shot at such close quarters. And, believe me, those Wots in the front were just sliced, there was no dodging, because their pals at the back were pressing them forward.

'There was another bit of fireworks going on round Temberly. Lucy came out of the port, slid around behind the mill the other two were making, and rushed for the man who was doing things to Temberly. Her fingers were crooked like claws as she came tearing at him. Lord, man, you should have seen his face when she'd finished – well, it just wasn't a face, that's all.

'Of course, it couldn't last. Somebody put a rifle stock in the way of Mackay's machete and knocked it out of his hand; even then it nearly decapitated another Wot as it flung free. Mackay still smiled. He doubled up his fists and started busting their jaws, but they piled on him and then got Freeman from the back. Some of them managed to grab Lucy, and then they'd got the lot of us – except Smith. Nobody had noticed him in the general dust-up. We thought he must still be in the *Fyra*, but one of the Wots gave a yell and pointed. There was Smith, he'd got through somehow and was legging it for the forest; he was mighty close to it, too. About six or seven Wots fired at once. That was the end of Smith, poor devil.

'We began to wonder what was the next ingenious little beastliness in the Wots' minds. It wasn't long before we found out.'

XI

RESCUE

Arrul, the Gorlak, led Knight and Hal forward unerringly. At times the growths became so thick that even the dimness overhead was blotted out, and they were forced to hold one another to keep together in the darkness.

'Can the Gorlaks see at night?' Hal asked.

'Very little better than we can, if at all, but they seem to have some warning sense of obstructions – I've seen blind men avoid things in the same way. The doctors say that it is due to sounds being reflected by the objects.'

They trudged monotonously on in silence. Hal was unable to see his watch, but it seemed certain that several hours had passed before they at last worked clear of the trees and stood on the edge of a large open space.

'That was very well done, Arrul,' Knight said. Turning to Hal he nodded:

'From here, we can phone Chicago to be ready.'

'From where?'

Knight pointed ahead. Hal gradually was able to make out the bulk of a huge building, so little darker than the sky which

146

backed it, as to be almost invisible. While they were hurrying forward, Knight drew a small whistle from his pocket and produced that same wailing note to which Arrul had earlier given answer. Some seconds later, doors in the building opened to emit a beam of light which momentarily dazzled the three. They ran forward, Knight calling to the men silhouetted in the opening. To Hal, the diminutive appearance of these guards gave a new idea of the scale of the building. Soon they passed in through a tall archway and the gates clashed behind them.

'Wait here a minute,' Knight said.

Hal watched him disappear through a small doorway, and then turned to study the surroundings with growing astonishment. It was evident, at once, that this was no single structure, but a whole town. The lighting was dim, for, as he guessed, the inhabitants were most of them asleep. But it showed enough for him to see that the buildings were arranged in concentric circles, and that he was standing between the two outer rings.

Straight ahead a large archway pierced the façade and through it he could see the road continuing for some distance, alternately dark and light, as it passed under more blocks or across more open spaces. Lights were showing here and there from scattered windows both in the ring before him, and in that through which they had entered. He was puzzled that no lights had been visible as they approached and asked Arrul the reason.

'Snipers,' said the Gorlak with his customary economy of speech.

The guardians of the gate had been regarding Hal with a deep interest. It was obvious that they knew him for a member of the rocket ship. One of them overheard his question, and volunteered information:

'Originally, we were never safe from the Wots. Our only method of preserving ourselves from their marauding bands was to wall our cities solidly, and leave no opening for bullets. The Wots were far bolder in the old days than they are now. A century ago this city had to stand sieges, but even now the walls are necessary, as the Gorlak said, to save us from being picked off by snipers. One could fight an army, but against sharpshooters . . . ' He completed the sentence with an expression of disgust.

Knight came hurrying back.

'I've got through to Chicago. They're getting things ready.

We ought to be able to get there before they start, if we hurry.'

The guards had wheeled out a long, low, black machine. As the two slipped into their seats, Knight turned to Arrul.

'Collect your people and wait for us,' he said.

Arrul nodded solemnly, and the car slid off towards the centre of the city.

'Straight road all the way to Chicago from the opposite gate,' Knight explained to the mystified Hal. 'We rarely go out of the cities at night, but we've got to risk Wot bullets this time.'

Their approach had evidently been signalled, so that the far gates stood open and ready for them to shoot out on to a broad highway. Knight crouched lower over the wheel and put his foot down. The machine was remarkably silent, and seemed to go like the wind. Hal remembered that the other had spoken of storage batteries as almost the only method of powering on Venus. As they sped through the night, he asked:

'Why don't you use radio? A portable transmitter would have saved us hours – in any case, I should have thought it was a necessity on this planet.'

'Won't work,' Knight replied, his eyes fixed on the road. 'Somebody's always got new ideas to make it possible, but they never work out. You see, we've not only got two or three reflecting layers, but reflecting curtains, as well. It would be easy if they were constant, but they're always shifting with temperature and climate. Apparently quite haphazardly – at least, no one yet has been able to predict their movements. Radio's worse than useless if it is ninety-nine per cent certain to let you down.'

Hal remembered his own transmitter's failure to raise the *Fyra* and nodded comprehendingly.

Knight, concentrating on driving, was quiet for a while, and Hal lay back in his seat to ease his weariness. He was almost dozing when the glare of lamps down the road startled him. Knight steered the black machine to one side, giving room to a row of heavy squat shapes.

'Tanks,' he said gleefully, 'they've not lost much time.' A few moments later he pointed ahead:

'Chicago.'

This time, it was no lightless city that they approached instead, the whole massive outer wall was bathed in a flood of whiteness.

Closer, Knight ran the car off the road, and sprang out. Hal followed, bewildered at the sight before him. The Dington forces were assembling for action.

The foreground was a scene of rushing activity, while behind, the wall of this new Chicago swept up in the floodlights like an enormous black cloth. Hal was struck with a sense of incongruity. In front of what might have been the ramparts of some medieval city, he could see tanks swiftly crawling from the huge main gateway on to the road. And, every now and again, a shadow as of a monstrous bat passed across the wall as one of the strange Venusian flying machines sank flapping, to take up its position in line. Everywhere there seemed to be a bustle and confusion, and a shouting of commands.

Knight hurried over to a group of officers and spoke for a few minutes, then he returned to Hal.

'That's fixed,' he said. 'They're letting us have a three-seater machine, and we start in ten minutes.'

The take-off of the ornithopter was a curious sensation for a rocket pilot. Knight first depressed a lever on the dashboard and there was a rapid fluttering of wings outside. The whole craft vibrated uncomfortably as it lifted and began to rise straight up. Looking left and right, Hal could see a long line of the machines churning the air in similar fashion. Down below, yet another detachment of tanks was streaming along the road.

'Looks as though your whole military force must be in this,' he said.

The other grinned.

'Most of it is, and feeling pretty sore, too. After all, we've waited for you for eight hundred years and we feel you've had a pretty poor reception.'

As he spoke, he leaned forward and made an adjustment. The shuddering of the machine stopped abruptly, for a moment it seemed to hang, then the wings slowly began to move again, this time with great, surging beats. Hal could see that at the bottom of their strokes, the tips reached well below the level of the landing gear, and he understood why the rapid, short movement had been necessary in rising. At first, the occupants were forced back in their seats as each heavy sweep forced the plane forward, but once the desired speed was attained they seemed to swim smoothly on in a silence broken only by a swishing which barely penetrated to the cabin.

'If we are going straight there, what about the tanks? They'll be far behind, won't they?' Hal asked.

'They aren't too slow on the road, though the forest will hold them back a bit. The Chicago tanks are really a reinforcement: those from the other cities ought to arrive much the same time as we do,' Knight explained. 'You know,' he added, 'your arrival has precipitated a proper war. Most of us have been waiting to have a slam at the Wots on a big scale for a long time; now we've got a cause which overrides all the peace party's protests.'

The sky was beginning to grow lighter. In the thick air of Venus, the dawn was a spectacle of rioting colour to make Earthly dawns a dull memory. Knight began to look worried. They were still some distance from the *Fyra*, and he was afraid of the things which might take place before they could arrive.

The day was nearly an hour old when they passed over the end of the road, and the city at which they had called in the darkness. They could see that the spaces between the concentric rings of buildings were filled with Dingtons who looked up, waving to the fliers as they passed. Faintly the sound of cheering rose to them and then dropped behind as they sped out over the forest. Knight pointed down to the lanes of crushed debris streaking the country below.

'The tanks are on ahead,' he said.

It seemed to Hal that they flew dangerously near the ground, but he found that all the other ornithopters were on the same level, and realised that, as the day grew warmer, visibility was shortening in a way which made spotting from altitude quite impossible. Already the two far wings of the aerial fleet could only be dimly seen.

Half an hour later they caught up the tanks. Hal had only received a distant impression of these during the night; now an exclamation escaped him as he gazed down. The machines were travelling on both wheels and tractor treads at a rate which was almost half that of the fliers. At the front of each projected two supports, holding what at first appeared to be a disc of bright metal. A nearer view showed it in reality to be a wheel of knife blades, revolving in the horizontal plane at high speed. By these devastating instruments, the soft growths were being swept away like melting butter, and the remains crushed to a dirty white pulp beneath the grinding tanks. Hal shuddered at the thought of the carnage should any of the

Wots attempt to obstruct the monsters' paths.

A blasting roar from somewhere not far ahead jerked him back to the matter in hand.

'Rockets,' he exclaimed. 'The *Fyra*'s rockets, what the devil are they doing?'

A moment later they reached the clearing and could see the glimmer of the ship's hull. As they swept towards the clustering Wots, Knight pressed his machine gun button. He purposely fired high for fear of hitting the prisoners, but the effect was instantaneous. Scared faces turned up for one glance at the descending fleet of ornithopters, and their owners scattered in every direction.

Scarcely a shot was fired in reply as the hundreds of Wots bounded for the safety of the forest. Several planes sank fluttering beside the *Fyra* where three bound figures stood; the rest hunted the fleeing Wots to the trees. From one side of the clearing rose shrieks of terror as the wretches found themselves trapped between the pursuing machine guns of the ornithopters and the deadly tanks breaking cover ahead. As the machine landed, Hal sprang out and ran towards his roped friends. He noticed that the *Fyra*'s port stood wide open, and a horrible fear gripped him.

'Where are the rest?' he demanded as he cut Temberly's bonds. 'Where's Vida?'

'Those devils have got her; carried off all three of the women,' said Crawshaw.

'And the men?'

'Dead, like we'd have been in another ten minutes,' Heerdahl replied.

'Which way did they take the women?' Knight asked.

'Over there,' Crawshaw pointed. 'A plane like one of these came along. They bundled them all three into it and flew off that way.'

'Damn them,' said Knight. 'I've always said that they'd got hold of some of those machines which were reported wrecked.'

He turned to an officer.

'Find accommodation in planes for these two men,' he directed, pointing to Crawshaw and Temberly. 'We'll take the other with us. Put some tanks on guard here. We've got to be quick. You two get aboard,' he added to Hal and Heerdahl.

Hal demurred momentarily.

'What about taking the *Fyra*?' he suggested.

Knight took his arm and urged him towards the ornithopter.

'No good for this job. Too big, and besides, you can't use your guns. Come along, time's precious.'

The great wings threshed furiously, and again the machine shuddered into the air.

XII

FINALE

The clearing slipped behind and they were able to catch glimpses through the trees of feverish activities proceeding below. There was the sound of intermittent rifle fire. Knight pointed down.

'Arrul and his people are on the job,' he said. 'There's many a Wot down there who wishes he had never developed a taste for roast Gorlak.'

'Good luck to Arrul – I'm with him altogether,' growled Heerdahl.

'Judging by the sight around the ship, you didn't do so badly yourselves,' Knight commented. 'I didn't count the Wot bodies, but there were plenty of them.'

'Not my doing, worse luck,' said Heerdahl. He went on to tell of the heroic fight of Mackay and Freeman, and the death of Smith.

'The next thing,' he continued, 'was the arrival of the flier and the kidnapping of the women – and there were we, each with a dozen Wots hanging on to us, and all tied up, too. It was hell. We couldn't do a thing but kick out, though we did that hard enough. After the plane had gone, they thought it was time to take it out of us, and started giving nasty looks at Freeman. He'd paid out a number of Wots in the scrap, and they weren't pleased about it – they weren't fond of Mackay either, but he had been disarmed a bit sooner than Freeman.

'Well, they held a bit of a talk and began to look so pleased with themselves that we knew something pretty beastly was in the wind. With nasty grins, they hauled Freeman away from the rest of us. First they ripped off his clothes, and then they

152

tied a rope to each of his ankles and wrists – that wasn't too easy: Freeman's were tough fists, but they did it, and started dragging him towards the stern of the *Fyra*. It was only then that we saw their idea, and we had to stand by and watch them tie poor Freeman across the rocket exhaust tubes. One of the Wots went into the ship.

'I guess Mackay just went mad then. God knows how he broke loose, but he did, and before we knew what was happening, he was on that crowd with a machete in each hand – carving at them with strokes which ripped them to bits. I've seen a few rough houses in my time, but Mackay's show made them all seem like petting parties. The Wots just melted away in front of him – those who didn't get sliced. I don't blame them, either. I know I'd have moved fast if I'd been faced with those two machetes and Mackay's grin behind them. He ploughed through the gang right up to where Freeman was spreadeagled over the tubes. He'd only time to slash one of the ropes through before the Wots were back at him and he had to turn on them.

'It was just then that the Wot executioner found the rocket keys. He couldn't see from the control desk what was happening back at the stern, so he just pressed.

'There was a gush of flame, with a roar which nearly split our ears, and the whole ship slid a couple of yards forward.'

Heerdahl paused a moment, then he added:

'When the smoke cleared, there was no sign of Mackay nor Freeman – they had been flashed out, and two dozen Wots with them. It was a mercifully quick end . . . A couple of minutes later, you turned up.'

For a time nobody spoke. Knight's look was grim as he pushed the ornithopter at top speed. Hal seemed to be staring blankly ahead, all expression wiped from his face. It was Heerdahl who felt that he must break the silence his own story had created.

'Where, exactly, are we heading?' he asked in a tone which strove to be normal.

'To the Wots' one town of any size,' Knight replied, catching the other's mood. 'It's called Ararat.'

'More traces of Watson – he was a Biblical old fellow, wasn't he? But I'd gathered that the Wots were more or less nomadic?'

'They are, mostly, but this is a sort of shrine in memory of Watson – their great religious meeting-place. Besides, they had to have some central manufacturing place for weapons and tools. Luckily they've never made more than small arms; it would need more organisation and control than they like, to go in for big guns.'

Hal broke in. There was a hard edge to his voice.

'Can't you get this damned thing to go any faster?'

'Flat out,' replied Knight shortly.

The field of vision was so limited that they found themselves passing over the outskirts of the Wots' city before they had realised that they were near the end of the journey. Roughly made, single-storey huts appeared among the trees, growing more numerous and more closely packed as they advanced. Soon they were looking down on twisting, narrow streets. The city of Ararat had more of the higgledy-piggledy imper-manence of a gold-rush town than the solidity of a nation's metropolis. Moreover not a solitary figure was to be seen in any of the roads.

'Where – ?' Hal began. Then a look of horror spread over his face.

They had reached an oval arena, packed with thousands of the semi-nude Wots. All were facing the far end, their heads bent down as though in prayer on a great block at the far end of the arena, was mounted the gigantic stone figure of a man. He was dressed in the clothes of a fashion long past, and was in the act of raising both hands to heaven, as though invoking.

'So they've made an idol of Watson,' Heerdahl murmured.

Hal did not hear. He was gazing at a form standing before the block, dwarfed into insignificance by the huge statue tower-ing above. From a metal collar about her neck, a chain led to a staple set in the stone. She saw the plane as it came, and lifted her arms in an imploring gesture. Simultaneously, the Wots seemed to break the spell which had held them. They flung back their arms, and a volley of stone flew through the air towards the lonely figure.

Knight slowed and banked steeply to bring his machine gun to bear. He could see a second plane, flying low over the crowd. He heard a great cry of 'Freda', and saw a man drop from it.

By all rights, Crawshaw should have killed himself in that rash leap, but he did not. He landed sprawling in the space which lay between the crowd and its victim. In a split second he was up and running towards Freda. She sank under the hail

154

of stones as he reached her. Crawshaw was flagging, something inside him had not stood the strain of that jump, but he reached the fallen girl and flung his own body across her as a shield.

Somewhere a rifle cracked. A spray of machine gun bullets answered and, as the other planes came up, each added its stream of lead. The Wots surged first one way and then the other, faltered, and then broke, trampling one another under foot in a wild dash for the safety of the narrow streets. Still the machine guns mercilessly followed them; the Dingtons were out for blood this time.

Knight landed his ornithopter near the towering statue of Watson. Hal walked slowly from it to the two who lay before the stone block.

The others saw him shake his head and then gently lay his coat over the clasped figures. He stood for a moment looking down upon them, before he turned to walk unsteadily back.

'They are both dead and they are both smiling,' he said quietly. 'I think I should like to die like that.'

'Hal,' a voice cried. Vida's voice.

Hal opened his mouth, but at first no sound came.

'Where are you, Vida?' he managed at last. His tone was curiously unsteady.

'In a cell under the statue.'

It was the work of a few minutes to free Vida and, with her, Lucy. Vida flung herself into her husband's arms and wept uncontrollably with relief.

Temberly bounded from a machine whose wings had scarcely ceased to flap and ran towards Lucy. Her eyes, too, were glistening wetly as they met.

'My dear – your head,' she cried.

But Temberly had forgotten the angry red weal across his brow. His heart had been aching more than his head. They forgot too the merciless slaughter of the Wots and their city of fanaticism as the machine guns and the rifles of the Gorlak hordes pressed on to the killing.

'Did you know that stoning was their punishment for blasphemy?' Heerdahl asked.

The other admitted it.

'I was afraid so. The Wots seem to be travelling a reverse path; very soon, they would have been true savages, perhaps below the level of the Gorlaks. We must kill them off now, all of them; else we will never feel safe.'

Heerdahl pondered in silence for a while, then:

'It's odd,' he said reflectively. 'Here are we, reaching out to the stars, while they sink back to the slime. Where does it all lead?'

Of the rest you know. Newspapers and films have shown you pictures of the Venusian life. Temberly's book, 'The Flora and Fauna of Known Venus', is a best seller. Most of poor Freda's salvaged pictures and notes have been published. Hal and Vida Newton have described both in print, and on the radio, the royal way in which the Dingtons treated their visitors when the *Fyra* was landed near that new and strange Chicago – all this is common knowledge.

My task has been, not to describe Venus, but to tell the story of her discoverers. And though five of those who set out have joined that glorious company of adventurers which has paid with its lives for the conquest of space; yet their memory is no less to be honoured than that of the four who returned and the one who remains. On? Yes, Heerdahl is still on Venus, helping Knight to build a second *Fyra*. Any day may see them come, roaring like a man-made meteor, towards the Earth.

JOHN WYNDHAM

STOWAWAY TO MARS

An international money prize was being offered to the first man to complete an interplanetary journey, and Dale Currance, the famous aircraft designer, volunteered as the British entrant. With a hand-picked crew, he blasted off from Salisbury Plain in his own spaceship, GLORIA MUNDI, destination – Mars. But once free of the Earth's atmosphere, he discovered a stowaway on board – a woman.

Joan and her strange quest should have prepared them better for the fantastic world that waited far out in the darkness of space. But the men from Earth were from a relatively young and hopeful civilisation, while Mars was a dying planet. Its inhabitants knew they could survive in one way only – a way too abhorrent for the Earthmen to comprehend. Only Joan realised they might have a lesson to learn from the Martian race. For one day Earth would die, too . . .

CORONET BOOKS

JACK VANCE

MARUNE

From his fabulous palace on Numenes, the Connatic ruled the sprawling Alastor Clustor . . . and kept track of the doings of each of his trillion or more subjects. But there was one man he knew nothing about – for the past life of the wanderer called Pardero was a complete mystery.

Pardero set himself two goals. To find out who he was . . . and to find his enemy, the person who had stolen his memory.

Psychologists deduced that his home world must be the mysterious Marune . . . a planet lit by four shifting suns. Pardero made his way there – and was hailed as the Kaiark Efraim, ruler of the shadowed realm.

Uncovering his lost identity had been comparatively simple. Finding his sworn enemy would be more difficult . . . there were so many people to choose from!

CORONET BOOKS

ROBERT SILVERBERG

SHADRACH IN THE FURNACE

The year is 2012. The world lies ravaged by biological warfare, its population decimated by a ferocious genetically-transmitted disease known as the organ rot. And presiding over the ruins is a ninety-three-year-old tyrant, preserved in a state of youth by a series of organ transplants: the self-styled Genghis Mao.

Shadrach Mordecai, Genghis Mao's trusted personal physician, was a vital cog in the great machine devoted to keeping the ruler alive: linked to him by a network of electronic implants, Shadrach was able to detect and diagnose the first signs of malfunction in his lord and master. But close as he was to the ageing dictator, Shadrach could not have known that events would soon plunge him into a desperated struggle – a struggle in which a paragon of idealism faced the very incarnation of evil.

CORONET BOOKS

MORE SCIENCE FICTION AVAILABLE
FROM CORONET BOOKS

JOHN WYNDHAM
☐ 15835 2	Stowaway to Mars	60p
☐ 17306 8	Wanderers of Time	60p
☐ 17326 2	Sleepers of Mars	75p

JACK VANCE
☐ 20820 1	The Gay Prince	60p
☐ 21251 9	Big Planet	65p
☐ 19827 3	The Anome	75p
☐ 19828 1	The Brave Free Men	75p
☐ 19830 3	The Asutra	75p
☐ 22950 0	Marune	75p

ROBERT SILVERBERG
☐ 21297 7	Born With The Dead	80p
☐ 21978 5	Unfamiliar Territory	90p
☐ 23235 8	Shadrach in the Furnace	85p

GEORGE R. R. MARTIN
☐ 22779 6	A Song For Lya	85p

All these books are available at your local bookshop or newsagent, or can be ordered direct from the publisher. Just tick the titles you want and fill in the form below.

Prices and availability subject to change without notice.

CORONET BOOKS, P.O. Box 11, Falmouth, Cornwall.

Please send cheque or postal order, and allow the following for postage and packing:

U.K. – One book 25p plus 10p per copy for each additional book ordered, up to a maximum of £1.05.

B.F.P.O. and EIRE – 25p for the first book plus 10p per copy for the next 8 books, thereafter 5p per book.

OTHER OVERSEAS CUSTOMERS – 40p for the first book and 12p per copy for each additional book.

Name ....

Address ....

....